And what can this place be?

High moor and wiry brush, Bolshevik bog, vast field of

Utter self-possession.

The MacDiarmid Memorandum

Poems by Alan Riach

Paintings by Alexander Moffat and Ruth Nicol

Scotland Street Press
EDINBURGH

First Published in the UK in 2023 by
Scotland Street Press
100 Willowbrae Avenue
Edinburgh EH8 7HU

All rights reserved
Poems Copyright © Alan Riach
Images Copyright © Alexander Moffat, Ruth Nicol and William Johnstone
Music Copyright © Ronald Stevenson

The right of Alan Riach to be identified as the author of this work has been asserted in accordance with section 77 of the Copyright, Designs and Patents Act 1988

A CIP record of this book is available from the British Library

ISBN 978-1-910895-79-5

Typeset and cover design by Mirrin Hutchison in Edinburgh
Cover image by Alexander Moffat
Back cover image by Ruth Nicol
Frontispiece by William Johnstone
All other images by Alexander Moffat and Ruth Nicol

Printed and bound by TJ Books Limited, Padstow, Cornwall

LOTTERY FUNDED

For Rae

'You can't write the kind of poetry I've written, or wanted to write, without love.'

— Hugh MacDiarmid

Contents

List of Paintings	x
Acknowledgements	xii
Foreword / Deirdre Grieve	xv
Introduction	1
A Border Boyhood / Langholm, Dumfriesshire	31
Three Rivers	32
The Learning	33
The Purchase of Tarras Moor	35
The Library	36
The Ministry of Water	37
The Border Guards	38
The Scottish Soul	40
World War I: Empires & small nations	41
Cultural Appropriation	42
Europe's far enough for me	43
Renaissance / Montrose, Angus	45
Vortex	46
Company	46
Home	46
Love & loss	48
Prelude to Shetland	49
MacDiarmid on Whalsay / Shetland	51
A Glass of Cold Water, Mid-Afternoon	52
Air Salt Stone	52
Valda and Michael	53
MacDiarmid on Whalsay / Ronald Stevenson	54
MI5	58
Technique and Ideation	58
With the Fisherman	61
Onwards	63

World War II: Fascism & populism	65
The lines of men	66
The World Language	68
The Brownsbank Years / Biggar, Lanarkshire	69
Cottage	71
The Seasons:	73
Winter	73
Spring and Summer	75
Autumn	79
The Drains	80
Milne's Bar	84
DSCH	86
The unthinkable (Aberfan and Vietnam)	88
YY & MacD, GU, Bute Hall	89
Brownsbank domesticity	90
Valda's poem	93
Tait's MacDiarmid	95
Afterwords	99
Coda	100
Elegy	101
MacDiarmid's Language	102
Notes	104
Biographies	120

List of Paintings

William Johnstone, 'Head of Poet' 1964, ink on paper, 12.5 x 9 cm Frontispiece, p.iv

Ruth Nicol, 'The Esk at Langholm' 2014, acrylic on board, 30 x 30 cm, p.30

Ruth Nicol, 'The Ewes and the Esk at Langholm' 2014, acrylic on board, 30 x 30 cm, p.34

Alexander Moffat, 'The Border Guards: William Johnstone, Hugh MacDiarmid and F.G. Scott' 2023, oil on canvas, 92 x 137 cm, p.39

Alexander Moffat, 'The Scottish Renaissance: William Johnstone, F.G. Scott and Hugh MacDiarmid' 2022, oil on canvas, 123 x 92 cm, p.44

Alexander Moffat, 'Hugh MacDiarmid and F.G. Scott' 2022, oil on canvas, 123 x 92 cm, p.47

Ruth Nicol, 'Whalsay, Shetland' 2014, acrylic on board, 30 x 30 cm, p.50

Ruth Nicol, 'Sodom, Shetland' 2014, acrylic on board, 30 x 30 cm, p.59

Ruth Nicol, 'Bains Beach, Lerwick' 2017, acrylic on card, 15 x 15 cm, p.60

Ruth Nicol, 'Lodeberrie, Lerwick' 2017, acrylic on card, 15 x 15 cm, p.62

Ruth Nicol, 'Brownsbank Cottage and Gardens in Spring' 2021, acrylic on board, 15 x 21 cm, p.70

Ruth Nicol, 'Winter Road to Biggar' 2021, acrylic on canvas, 100 x 100 cm, p.72

Ruth Nicol, 'Through the Trees: A Spring Garden at Brownsbank Cottage' 2021, acrylic on board, 15 x 21 cm, p.74

Ruth Nicol, 'Through the Trees: A Summer Garden at Brownsbank Cottage' 2021, acrylic on board, 15 x 21 cm, pp.76-77

Ruth Nicol, 'Valda's Garden with Blue Gate' 2021, acrylic on board, 21 x 15 cm, p.78

Ruth Nicol, 'Everything You Could Need: The Kitchen Extension at Brownsbank Cottage' 2021, acrylic on board, 30 x 30 cm, p.81

Alexander Moffat, 'Milne's Bar' 2021, oil on canvas, 81 x 152 cm, pp.82-83

Alexander Moffat, 'Passacaglia on DSCH: Ronald Stevenson, p.87

Alexander Moffat, 'Valda and Chris' 2020, oil on canvas, 61 x 91 cm, p.92

Ruth Nicol, 'Wally Dugs, Warmth and a Welcome Hearth: Valda's Room at Brownsbank Cottage' 2021, acrylic on board, 30 x 30 cm, p.94

Ruth Nicol, 'Awards, Wally Dug, Jug and Rowan Tree: MacDiarmid's Room, Brownsbank Cottage' 2021, acrylic on board, 30 x 30 cm, p.97

Alexander Moffat, 'Hugh MacDiarmid: Brownsbank' 1978, oil on canvas, 91.5 x 58 cm, p.98

Alexander Moffat, 'Hugh MacDiarmid' 1978, charcoal and pastel on paper, 36 x 47.5 cm, p.103

Acknowledgements

Many thanks go to: Deirdre Grieve, Dorian Grieve, and in fact all the Grieves and all their families, and Nancy Gish, Alexander Linklater, Alexander Moffat, Ruth Nicol, the late Ronald Stevenson and Eddie McGuire, Fiona Paterson, my students and colleagues of over forty years in the Department of Scottish Literature at the University of Glasgow and many other universities around the world, poets and friends, Camille Manfredi, Peter McCarey, Denham MacDougall, James Robertson, Margaret Pool and the Tarras Valley Nature Reserve and all involved in the Langholm Initiative, Ron Addison, Fiona Stafford, Patrick Crotty, the late Lillias Scott Chisholm, Christopher Guild, Jamie Reid-Baxter, Ian Burnside, Andrew McNeillie, Ann Matheson, the late Marshall Walker, Gerry Cambridge, editor of *The Dark Horse*, in which three of these poems first appeared, Rod Hunt and the staff of the Scottish Poetry Library, Edinburgh, the University of Connecticut and the estate of the late Charles Olson, and the National Galleries of Scotland and the Estate of William Johnstone for permission to reproduce his 'Head of Poet' (1964) as the frontispiece to this book. I had the pleasure of meeting Johnstone at his retrospective exhibition in the Hayward Gallery on the South Bank in London in 1981. When I told him I was working for a PhD on Hugh MacDiarmid he beamed up at me from his wheelchair and declared, 'That's a terrible thing to be doing!' We happily agreed.

Thanks especially to my publisher Jean Fraser, and to Alex Strouts, for proof-reading and editing, and Mirrin Hutchison, for typesetting and book design, and for all the investment, keen-eyed insights and suggestions, patient exploration of possibilities and confirmation of the best way possible to present the material from which this book has been composed.

The sources for some of the quotations, phrases or observations in the Introduction and in the poems themselves include Philip Larkin, *Selected Letters 1940-1985*, edited by Anthony Thwaite (London: Faber, 1992), Kingsley Amis, *The Letters*, edited by Zachary Leader

(London: Harper Collins, 2000); and more importantly, Alan Bold, *MacDiarmid: Christopher Murray Grieve* (1988); Hugh MacDiarmid's essays 'The Chapbook Programme' (1922), 'Art and the Unknown' (1926), the little book *Albyn or Scotland and the Future* (1927), the essay 'Scotland: Full Circle' (1971); and his poems, *To Circumjack Cencrastus* (1930), 'The Ministry of Water', 'Water Music', *In Memoriam James Joyce* (1955); *Dear Grieve: Letters to Hugh MacDiarmid (C.M. Grieve)*, edited by John Manson (Glasgow: Kennedy & Boyd, 2011); and C.K. Stead, 'What I Believe', in *The Writer at Work: Essays* (2000). Further details of specific debts are in the NOTES. All the poems have been created within what MacDiarmid called 'a strong solution of books' but not only that: music, films, paintings, newspapers, television and radio reportage, other poems, and songs. Nor are they only what were called once 'intertexts'. If they're any good at all, they're more than that.

For the exhibition *Landmarks*:

For all their support with the exhibition, Alexander Moffat, Ruth Nicol and Alan Riach would like to thank the directors of the Lillie Gallery (Milngavie), the Montrose Museum and Art Gallery, the Junor Gallery (St Andrews), the Biggar and Upper Clydesdale Museum, the Line Gallery (Linlithgow), the Scottish Storytelling Centre (Edinburgh), MacDiarmid's Brownsbank and the Saltire Society.

Alexander Moffat's *Poets' Pub* is in the Scottish National Portrait Gallery. See:
https://www.nationalgalleries.org/art-and-artists/8217/poets-pub

Ruth Nicol's *Holyrood, 2014: The Scottish Parliament* is in the Scottish Parliament building at Holyrood. See:
https://www.parliament.scot/visitandlearn/88978.aspx

An earlier version of the essay 'Landmarks: Hugh MacDiarmid's Brownsbank – Paintings by Alexander Moffat and Ruth Nicol, Poems by Alan Riach' (part of which is revised in the Introduction to the present book) can be found on the website of Hugh MacDiarmid's Brownsbank: See http://www.macdiarmidsbrownsbank.org.uk/ The quotation from Michael Grieve towards the end of the Introduction is from *The Glasgow Herald* (10 September 1988); the final phrase in the quotation is from the opening paragraph of *The Scotsman*'s editorial (11 September 1978), where the verb was present tense.

Foreword

The extraordinary life which Alan Riach traces in this cycle of poems began in the beautiful Border town of Langholm, a town I first saw in the early months of marriage in 1958 to Michael Grieve, son of Christopher Grieve and his second wife, Valda. Shortly before the wedding I opened a letter from a cousin working in Nigeria and drew out a handsome cheque towards, she thought, furnishings for a marital home. 'I'll have that,' said the bridegroom plucking it from my fingers. And in the space of two weeks he had bought an elderly 2.5 litre Jaguar, light blue with leather upholstery and windows that didn't quite close, booked, sat and passed a driving test, and driven us forty miles to Brownsbank cottage, still in its primitive state, untouched by *Star Wars* (see Alan's poem, 'The Drains'), The Force not yet with it, hence the storm lantern, Calor Gas heater and chemical toilet in the back garden, a telephone directory on a loop of string for loo paper, and no phone to tell his father he now had wheels and could take him anywhere.

And so one weekend Chris, Valda, Mike and I went to Langholm. Over the years Chris had largely lost contact with his place of birth, but had mentioned it occasionally, not always favourably, and his long, best-known poem, *A Drunk Man Looks at the Thistle*, is set there. In his late sixties he had no idea how, if at all, he would be remembered there. Mike parked the Jaguar at Chris's direction, outside one of the hotels on the High Street, the Eskdale or the Crown, and we walked into the public bar where an elderly man sitting at the bar looked round, said 'Aye, Kit' and returned to his pint. Whether he knew him or not Chris returned the greeting, and Valda, Mike and I logged into the place in our heads that filed facts from the extraordinary life and added a new and improbable nick name to the list.

Over the years we went back many times, Chris re-established contact with relatives and on several occasions we went to the Common Riding which features in *A Drunk Man*. An all-day event echoed in other Border towns, the Common Riding recreates the marching of the borders that in its early days preserved the town's land rights, in Langholm's case featuring: a proclamation, 'The Crying of the Fair', from a man standing on the back of a horse, marching bands and perhaps a hundred horses, clattering and snorting with riders of all ages. Utterly spectacular is the horseback charge up a vertiginous paved hill, inches from the spectators who line the verges, the horses wild-eyed, muscles bunched and flexed, limbs and torsos stretched, embodiments of power and terrifying, their riders magnificent in alpha plus control, insuperable. On my last visit to the Common Riding, my companions on the verge of the horse charge were three men, all tall, well-built, alpha-tending in matters of the intellect and all well-versed in the poetry and the biography of Christopher Grieve. As the last horses thundered past, they turned to each other, rocked by sheer shared contextual inadequacy and simultaneously clobbered by enlightened fellow feeling. For this was what a male child growing up in Langholm would be measured against. The alternative, the laundry baskets full of books brought from the library – the 'brain-washing' of Alan's poem – was the road out of Langholm and into the wider world.

But while for Christopher Grieve, morphing into Hugh MacDiarmid, the world of the intellect and the circles which came with that world grew ever wider, the places he lived in – after one world war, a long productive time in Montrose and a taxing time in London – shrank dramatically, first to the Shetland island of Whalsay where Valda came into her own, honing survival skills for a family without regular income with discarded fish, seagulls' eggs, peat digging and hand knitting, then finally to Biggar, and the long, happy and tranquil period Alan visits in 'The Brownsbank Years', remote enough to avoid time-wasting visitors but a sanctuary and place of welcome for friends old and new.

Our sons, when small, loved to stay, one at a time, with their grandparents, where they were given dangerous tasks by Valda involving logs, a saw, roofing felt and tar and dogs to be walked avoiding sheep. The cottage seemed to swell when visitors arrived, from all over the world. One memorable visit was from Garech Browne, commonly tagged in newspapers as a Guinness Heir, who had recorded Chris reading his poems for his Claddagh Records. He came with his beautiful wife Purna, a princess, daughter of a maharajah, who cooked an amazing Indian meal for us in the cottage's tiny kitchen. A kitchen built, along with the bathroom, by students from Edinburgh University and members of the Young Communist League, including the daughter of Alex McCrindle, best known as General Dodonna in *Star*

Wars, after the General himself had dug the necessary ditches.

The seasons as Alan pictures them, marked and often extreme for people living in two rooms on a rural hillside, brought gifts of gooseberries and broad beans grown in the small garden, and in winter some memorable journeys. One Sunday, arriving for lunch after a heavy overnight snowfall, we left the car at the bottom of the track which was clearly impassable. Mike settled our first small son on his shoulders and we battled up in thigh-high snow, sometimes blown off our feet by a gust of wind. Valda opened the door to us, gasping and snow-encrusted, with a country-woman's contempt for city-dwellers. 'Why didn't you come up across the field?' she said, pointing to the shallow coating of snow on the winter grazing, the night's snowfall contained in the deep drifts we had struggled through. Then we sat down to hot platefuls of her trademark delicious soup which she never failed to tell us was made from leavings on previous visitors' plates.

Alan Riach's sequence of poems don't all go into such domestic detail but some evoke or describe it accurately. Overall, they are a series of insights, biographical snapshots and meditations on moments in the life of my father-in-law, including, as well as poetry and the natural world, cultural and political priorities, friends and family and matters of personality. Read in sequence, they open a new approach to their sometimes elusive subject and make up an appreciation that is appropriate, challenging and engaging all the way through.

Deirdre Grieve, 2023

The MacDiarmid Memorandum: An Introduction

The poems that make up *The MacDiarmid Memorandum* are moments, episodes, encounters, events, hopefully illuminations, in the trajectory of a life, an arc of droplights across a stage, or torchlights washing over, pausing at some places on, as he put it, 'a statue carved out in a whole country's marble'. Curve by curve, by muscle and sinew, on skin, the bone beneath, the spine, the clay grown tall, places where the lungs take breath, the heart beats still, the voice flows forth, unfaltering.

My title remembers a novel and film from the mid-1960s, *The Quiller Memorandum*, written by Adam Hall and published in 1965; the film followed in 1966, with a screenplay by Harold Pinter. I was nine years old when my father took me to see it in the cinema. I think there's no harm in bringing in a text from popular culture that has some ironic poignancy, for it also deals with serious matters: neo-Nazis, post-Second World War fascism, rising again. It's never really gone away. We set ourselves against it.

Nobody set themselves against it more than Hugh MacDiarmid, poet, journalist, cultural revolutionary. With a fierce commitment to political change and a love of the Scots language and extremism of all sorts, he was the inspirational figure at the head of the Scottish Renaissance of the 1920s. He helped found the National Party of Scotland, galvanised all his contemporaries, making more enemies than friends, and wrote a lifetime of work including *A Drunk Man Looks at the Thistle* (1926), *Stony Limits* (1935) and *In Memoriam James Joyce* (1955). George Orwell included his name on the list he made for MI5 of people 'who should not be trusted'. MacDiarmid's impact in his day and even now was and is charged with a dynamic power that rebukes authority and yet commands it. His writing could be scintillating and skilful, witty and determined, outwardly directed propaganda, of one kind or another, or deeply introspective.

> 'Let there be Licht,' said God, and there was
> A little: but He lacked the poo'er

> To licht up mair than pairt o' space at aince,
> And there is lots o' darkness that's the same
> As gin He'd never spoken
>   – Mair darkness than there's licht,
> And dwarfin't to a candle-flame,
> A spalin' candle that'll sune gang oot.
> – Darkness comes closer to us than the licht,
> And is oor natural element. We peer oot frae't
> Like cat's een bleezin' in a goustrous nicht
> (Whaur there is nocht to find but stars
> That look like ither cats' een),
> Like cat's een, and there is nocht to find
> Savin' we turn them in upon oorsels;
> Cats canna.

Poetry like this goes beyond all that preceded it. MacDiarmid transformed what Scottish literature – and politics – might be. He was a one-man demolition squad attacking the establishment.

This is a book of poems in response to MacDiarmid's life, a full-length sequence tracking him from his boyhood in Langholm, in the Scottish Borders, through the violent vortex of post-First World War modernist artistic revolution in Montrose, across the ending of his first marriage and into his 'internal exile' in the Shetland Islands in the 1930s with his second wife Valda and their young son Michael, and then later the move to Brownsbank Cottage, Biggar, from 1951 till his death in 1978. It's a mosaic biography in verse, taking us on a lyrical trajectory following the central figure in Scotland's 20th-century cultural life, delivering a compassionate depiction of a volatile yet vulnerable man, from childhood to old age: a beacon undimmed.

2022 marked one hundred years since the name Hugh M'Diarmid first appeared in print. Since 1992, I've been trying to make his work more available, in Scotland and internationally. Since that year, when Carcanet began publishing MacDiarmid's collected works under my General Editorship, his readership has grown and diminished and grown again; his impact has been recognised, scorned, returned to and for many, secured. 'We must get him out of the hands of the Scots!' one early piece of advice was given to me. We must put him back into the hands and minds of new generations, I replied.

Back in 1992, there was some thought that a small anthology of the early poems in Scots might be published but as I recall, nothing – in that 70th anniversary year – was actually in print and available. Nothing. The thirty years from 1992 to 2022 changed that, at least. I remember on Orchard Road in Singapore, in the big Kinokuniya bookshop in the mid-1990s, seeing a row of the Carcanet edition on the shelves. The *Selected Poems,* paperbacked in Penguin Modern Classics and published in America by New Directions, is kept available by Carcanet and is a set text in universities. Another comment I remember from that time was the English poet and university don Jeremy Prynne, on the phone to me from Cambridge, saying, when I told him of what I was intending to do to bring MacDiarmid back into print: 'Well, he's not going to go away, is he?'

Jonathan Bate, in his book *Radical Wordsworth: The Poet Who Changed the World* (London: William Collins, 2020) says this: 'The role of literary as opposed to historical biography should be to discern and seek to explain the distinctive qualities of the subject's imaginative power. Why else should one bother to write, or read, the life of a poet?' This book is not a 'literary biography' but it shares something of the same purpose.

Besides, there is more than one biography. There is the singular person, Christopher Murray Grieve, then there is the poet and writer Hugh MacDiarmid, and you could follow two stories, one in literary criticism, tracking what is there to read, and another in the mortal life. Yet the two are not really, ultimately, separable. The poems in this book elide them. Whatever physical, emotional and imaginative experience was gone through by C.M. Grieve was essential source material for Hugh MacDiarmid. And MacDiarmid takes us so much further.

Bate also supplies a quotation from Gerald Haylett, from the *New Chronicle*, 27 January 1937, referring to James Frazer, author of *The Golden Bough* (1890): 'Though but few have read the work by which he lives, and fewer know more of him than his name, he has changed the world… He has changed it by altering the chemical composition of the cultural air that all men breathe.' Bate says this accords with his sense of Wordsworth's influence. I'd say the same of MacDiarmid.

A Personal Encounter

I met him in the last years of his life but my reading of him began at my secondary school, in Gravesend, in Kent, deep in darkest south-east England, of all places, when the Headmaster, James Brogden, asked me if I'd read this poet, living now, writing in the language of Scotland, the nation where I was born, from which I had come to this school in the south of England. I had not. He told me I should. A teacher, Chris Botten, then introduced me to the poetry of Robert Henryson, the 15th-century Scots Makar whose masterwork, 'The Testament of Cresseid', I studied for the entrance exam for Cambridge University in the little Penguin Books edition edited by MacDiarmid and published in 1973.

In the summer of 1976, I was in the old John Smith's bookshop in St Vincent Street in Glasgow, picked up a copy of the lovely pocket-sized 200 Burns Club edition of *A Drunk Man Looks at the Thistle* and opened it and my eyes widened and my brain went into fast acceleration mode. Here was a verse fluent and driving, in a language I knew from cousins, uncles, aunts, grandparents and friends, and it was dealing with matters of adult sexuality and politics and spirit. I was nineteen years old. I wanted to read more.

Later that summer I found the address of the publisher William MacLellan, on Garnethill in Glasgow, near the School of Art. I went there and knocked on the door. Bill's wife, the concert pianist Agnes Walker, opened it and let me in. Bill was sitting in his armchair by the fireplace, pipe in hand, dressed in kilt and grey tweed jacket, with a high pile of copies of MacDiarmid's *In Memoriam James Joyce* stacked beside him, as if he was guarding them. A couple of small Scottie dogs bounced around energetically. I asked if I might buy a copy of the book, and did, for £4.95. (It was the second edition from 1956.) That weekend, in my grandparents' home, in Calderbank, near Airdrie, in Lanarkshire, I sat down and read it, cover to cover. That was a different kind of exhilaration: a hunt that started then that's never ended.

The following year, at Cambridge, my tutor, Tim Cribb,

who had met and knew MacDiarmid and Valda, told me that if I was enthusiastic about his work I should go and visit him, he would welcome that, and he wasn't getting any younger.

One late afternoon a fellow-student friend named Chris Larsen and I decided that the time had come. We set off, hitch-hiking overnight from Cambridge to Edinburgh. The next day, one of my uncles took us by car to Biggar, we found Brownsbank Cottage after various enquiries and wrong roads, and Chris and I went up and knocked on the door. As we were waiting, we saw the old man sitting by the window in Valda's room, watching a rugby match on the TV in the near corner. Valda answered the door and fiercely demanded to know who we were. Bona fides somewhat shyly offered, knowing we were risking rudeness, 'Well, you'd better come in,' she said, and admitted us. The conversation continued in further visits through those last years of MacDiarmid's life, and with Valda, after his death. That conversation too has never really ended.

There's a Thames Television programme I watched when it was first broadcast in 1977 and again more recently on YouTube, 'People and Politics', in which, about 20 minutes in, MacDiarmid is invited to speak. This is the year I met him first, the year before his death and two years before the 1979 referendum on Scottish devolution (March 1st), which most voters in Scotland approved only for the result to be torpedoed by a Labour party minister at Westminster. Shortly after that (May 3rd), Margaret Thatcher's Conservative government came into power with a majority of votes in England. This is what MacDiarmid says in 1977: 'I've got no interest whatever in devolution of any kind at all, of any degree. I want Scottish independence, and ultimately a Scottish Republic. That's not a new idea. But the majority of the Scottish people don't want that. The majority of the Scottish people don't know any more than they've ever known what they want. In any case, they couldn't want what I stand for because until quite recently, Scottish schools, colleges and universities had no courses in Scottish literature or the Scottish languages. They were entirely conditioned by English standards. I want to break away from all that. I want complete disjunction from England…'

In other words, poetry, the work of all the arts, is a major fact of any society, but no less important politically is education, the work of all people, but particularly educational institutions, all of them, and the politicians charged with helping make such education happen. That was the imperative MacDiarmid set. In that programme, in 1977, he said, 'until quite recently…' Let's remind ourselves of the establishment of the Association for Scottish Literary Studies in 1970 and of the Department of Scottish Literature at the University of Glasgow in 1971. He knew what he was talking about.

If MacDiarmid insisted on drawing the line between Scotland and England, it's not hard to find an English response. Here's Philip Larkin writing about MacDiarmid on 2 April 1971 in a letter to Dan Davin at Oxford University Press about Larkin's editing *The Oxford Book of Twentieth Century English Verse*: 'I am so averse from his work that I can hardly bring my eyes to the page, but I agree a lot of people will expect to find him there (assuming, of course, that he will consent to be included in a work whose title includes the word English) and if you like I will make another effort to find some stretch of his verbiage that seems to me a trifle less arid, pretentious, morally repugnant and aesthetically null than the rest.' Kingsley Amis, in a letter to the poet Robert Conquest on 28 October 1976, after having hosted a TV show and introduced MacDiarmid on it, was more succinct: 'Off his head, of course.'

Nor was there any lack of critics at home. Ian Hamilton Finlay, who had been a young friend of MacDiarmid and Valda in Glasgow, and at whose first wedding MacDiarmid had been best man, came squarely into the older poet's sights when he became one of a group opposed to the selection MacDiarmid's friend Norman MacCaig had made for his anthology *Honour'd Shade: An Anthology of New Scottish Poetry to mark the Bicentenary of the Birth of Robert Burns* (Edinburgh: Chambers, 1959). In response to the critique of MacCaig, MacDiarmid published a vitriolic little essay as a pamphlet, *the ugly birds without wings* (Edinburgh: Allan Donaldson, 1962). When I visited Ian Hamilton Finlay at Stonypath, at his home by his playful, provocative, gentle and chilling garden, Little Sparta, courtesy of his son Alec, Ian knew of my work on MacDiarmid and my admiration and liking for it. He took me out to the porch overlooking the green fields of Lanarkshire, pointed to a small hill on the horizon, a little way beyond which was the town of Biggar, and beyond that, Brownsbank. He pointed to it and smiled and said, 'Do you see that, Alan? That is the MacDiarmid Alp.' It was a comment simultaneously funny, fierce, friendly and bristling.

My personal story of encountering MacDiarmid and his work overlaps with the last years of his life and the rise of neoliberal economics internationally and emphatically within the UK, and the political structures that have continued to hold Scotland in a judicial trap. We're still trying to free ourselves. The work of poetry and all the arts, as MacDiarmid demonstrated, is no use as a panacea, nor as compensation, nor therapy, and it's certainly no guarantee of economic growth. That it should be seen as such is a very silly notion. Above all, it's no good if it doesn't touch what humanity is at its best, what human potential is at its fullest, for it can equally show what we're like at our worst. And for over 100 years that's what MacDiarmid has been teaching us to understand.

Landmarks: The Exhibition

This is the history from which the poems in this book began to be composed. The first of them were collected for display as part of an exhibition, *Landmarks: Poets, Portraits and Landscapes of Modern Scotland.* This had its first airing at the Lillie Gallery, Milngavie, in 2018, going then to Montrose Museum and Art Gallery, and then the Junor Gallery in St Andrews. It was a showcase of some of the major poets of the 20th century, including Hugh MacDiarmid, Somhairle MacGill-Eain / Sorley MacLean, Robert Garioch, Edwin Morgan, George Mackay Brown, Sydney Goodsir Smith, Iain Mac a' Ghobhainn / Iain Crichton Smith, and Norman MacCaig.

My poems were to be printed simply and attractively on card and hung on the gallery walls beside the two interconnected sets of paintings, portraits by Alexander Moffat, and landscapes of the distinctive territories favoured by the poets by Ruth Nicol. The story of the exhibition should be noted here as well.

In the first instance, Sandy had painted the portraits of these poets in the late 1970s and early 1980s. He had first visited MacDiarmid at Brownsbank Cottage in the same year as I had, though neither of us knew the other at the time. After consultation and discussion with Sandy, in the 2010s, Ruth Nicol began her project of painting the landscapes these poets had favoured, whether they were born there or chose them to live in. Then Sandy and Ruth approached me with the idea that a set of poems might go along with their paintings and be essential to the exhibition.

So often, people visiting galleries pause only a few moments before each painting, and then move on. We thought that if they stopped long enough to read the poems, be hooked by them, they might look again at the paintings and see more in them. And more than that: Ruth's paintings were made not only of terrains and territories but also of towns and villages, buildings, homes, places inhabited and lived in, now. Sometimes they envision expansive landscapes, wide-screen paintings with vectors of distance and powerlines arcing over them and roads running through them. Sometimes they are smaller works, more intimate in detail. These places were and are now home to new generations of people, years and decades since the poets were there. What are the living generations to do with their poets of the past?

On the A7 approach road to Langholm at both ends of the town, there's a sign devised by the local school children: not 'Welcome to Langholm!' but rather: 'Slow down – Here comes Langholm – Birthplace of Hugh McDiarmid'.

We wondered about bringing in a sample of poems by the poets themselves. That would have further enhanced their iconic stature and there is nothing wrong with that, but one of the virtues of Sandy's portraits was the revelation of the fact that these were actual living people, not just words on pages. They were men, sons and fathers, husbands, members of communities of various sorts, clansmen of a kind. They lived in domesticity, their marriages and close friendships were, as all are, singular and unalike. What do poets' kitchens look like? What are the books on their shelves? Not to diminish their work, but to help understand the actuality of their lives, to humanise them. How poor some were, how relatively few were relatively prosperous. My poems might reflect upon these questions, maybe give some answers, speculations, or focus on an urgency, some pressing fact that still stays with us now.

Each iteration of the show highlighted different poets and their favoured places, and different emphases of argument were engaged. The centrepiece of the Junor Gallery exhibition in St Andrews was Sandy's major painting of 2017, *Scotland's Voices*, which widened the focus to include traditional musicians and singers, alongside the literary titans of modern Scotland. This revised the story presented in Sandy's earlier, iconic work, *Poets' Pub* (1980), and demonstrated that 'popular' and 'intellectual' arts need not be in opposition but rather inform and nourish each other. In a political climate where divide and rule has been common, this inclusiveness of vision is essential.

Biggar and Upper Clydesdale Museum, through the charitable trust MacDiarmid's Brownsbank, proposed to host a new configuration of the exhibition in 2020, but when the world was swept by the tidal wave of the Coronavirus pandemic, the first presentation of our work had to be online. Through the year that followed, many new works, portraits, landscapes and poems, were composed with this new iteration in prospect.

Hugh MacDiarmid was at the centre of this new presentation of *Landmarks* and the exhibition charted his later life, illustrating some of the encounters he had with other major artists – poets, singers, composers and others – throughout that long trajectory.

During the Brownsbank years, MacDiarmid, or, to acknowledge his domestic name, Chris (Christopher Murray Grieve) and his wife Valda (Valda Trevlyn Grieve), lived in the little two-room cottage a few miles east of Biggar. This period was our central focus.

Before Brownsbank, MacDiarmid's landscapes had pre-eminently been those of the Borders, of Langholm, in Dumfriesshire, then Montrose, where he was at the centre of the Scottish Renaissance movement of the 1920s, and then the small island of Whalsay in the Shetland archipelago. He moved from one extreme southernmost edge of Scotland to the northernmost, furthest away from it. His life was dedicated to bringing out the best from all that those two locations encompassed.

After Biggar in 2021, a smaller selection from the exhibition was shown in the Line Gallery in Linlithgow in 2022, marking the M'Diarmid centenary year. In November 2022, another selection of work was shown at the Scottish Storytelling Centre in Edinburgh but all along the sequence of poems relating to MacDiarmid had been growing, accumulating, and a sense that rather than see them in the context of the gallery exhibitions or the catalogue-books that we produced to go with them, they might be read as poems in their own priority, with a selection of the paintings there to complement and counterpoint the words.

Then a further thought approached: in 2004 the composer Ronald Stevenson (1928-2015), a trusted friend and great enabler of artists of all kinds, who had set a number of MacDiarmid's poems to piano accompaniment, surprised and delighted me by setting a poem of my own, evoking Chris Grieve with Valda and their son Michael, in Shetland, on Whalsay. Might that setting be printed in the book, to go with the poems and images, so that it could be played from the page on a piano, and sung, perhaps, if anyone should choose to do so? It might, indeed. So here we have the arts, triumvirate: poems, paintings, music, and with reference in my poem 'Tait's MacDiarmid' to the 1964 film-portrait made by the Orcadian poet and experimental director Margaret Tait, the medium of film is also invoked. But in this book, the poems lead the way.

They are all illustrations of a life. They can stand on their own as invitations, as all such poems are, to go further. But they are hopefully also complementary to the more fully-detailed personal biographies, Gordon Wright's *MacDiarmid: An Illustrated Biography* (1977), an invaluable compendium of photographs and text, the introductory chapter of Nancy K. Gish's *Hugh MacDiarmid: Man and Poet* (1984), Alan Bold's expansive, pioneering work *MacDiarmid: Christopher Murray Grieve* (1988), and the new biography by Alexander Linklater. Knowing the life story might make the poems easier but isn't a requirement. Yet as the great American poet William Carlos Williams once said, 'You should never explain a poem – but it always helps!' So however oblique or self-explaining the poems in this book may be, perhaps they do demand some further information about the life that prompted them. Here it is.

Langholm, Montrose and Shetland

Christopher Murray Grieve was born and grew up in the town of

Langholm, eight miles away from England. The small town is at the confluence of three rivers, the Wauchope, the Esk and the Ewes, and MacDiarmid later wrote that he could tell exactly where he was in Langholm simply by listening to the sound of the rivers. Their moving waters each had a different music. He writes of 'the honey-scented heather hills' and the forests and moors surrounding the town, in which he wandered and explored as a boy. But his love extended from the natural world of rivers, hills and forests to the other end of the spectrum, to book-learning. His father was the local postman and the family lived below the town library. He claimed that when he left Langholm he had read every single book in that library and knew what was in each one of them. So book-learning and the natural world were there from the start. And there was the annual Common Riding, the traditional summer festival 'Riding of the Marches', when a large company of horsemen and horsewomen ride around the boundaries of the countryside of Langholm's territory in a tradition centuries old, marking the border of their own provenance. In later life, MacDiarmid returned for it as often as he could.

He enlisted and saw service during the First World War in Salonika in Greece, in France and in the Pyrenees, as a Quarter Master Sergeant in the Royal Army Medical Corps. He was invalided out with cerebral malaria and demobbed in 1919. MacDiarmid spent the 1920s with his first wife Peggy and their children Walter and Christine, mainly in Montrose, on the east coast of Scotland, as a working journalist on the *Montrose Review*, but his first commitment then was to galvanise into dynamic life the Scottish Renaissance, a new movement in all the arts – poetry, literature, painting, sculpture, music – and to politicise the nation's consciousness of the prospect of an independent Scotland, on the world stage. He defines that commitment with a poetic conviction that reaches beyond the miserable world of petty party politics and really throws down the gauntlet in a short poem called 'Separatism':

> If there's a sword-like sang
> That can cut Scotland clear
> O' a' the warld beside
> Rax me the hilt o't here,

> For there's nae jewel till
> Frae the rest o' earth it's free,
> Wi' the starry separateness
> I'd fain to Scotland gie.

The worst implications of exceptionalism are challenged here by the dazzling appeal of language and metaphor: both the energy of 'Rax me the hilt o't here' and the beauty of 'starry separateness' are verbally persuasive beyond the clod-bound correctnesses upon which mundane politics insists. And it's true. Stars are beautiful in their separateness, and in their moving places in a constellation, what MacDiarmid calls elsewhere 'an aching spargosis of stars' (a 'spargosis' being the bulging distention of breasts filled with milk). The continuity is there in the vision of an independent self-determined nation in which there is room for difference and dialogue, full of potential nourishment and threatening no enforcement of sterile conformity. And there is no Supreme Court higher than poetry.

That idea of regeneration is essential. Renaissance is the word. In the spring of 1895, the sociologist, town planner and biologist Patrick Geddes published an essay entitled 'The Scots Renascence' in his periodical *The Evergreen*, declaring the prospect of a self-determined 'Renascence' in Scotland which would engage the cultural and political desire for liberation from 19th-century Anglocentrism and British imperialism. The title of Geddes's journal was a direct reference to Allan Ramsay's anthology of 1724, *The Ever Green*, itself followed by David Dalrymple, *Lord Hailes's Ancient Scottish Poems* (1770) and John Pinkerton's *Ancient Scottish Poems, Never Before in Print but now published from the MS. Collections of Sir Richard Maitland... comprising pieces written from about 1420 till 1586* (1786). These books republished poems from the 16th century and earlier, regenerating an awareness of a longer tradition of Scottish literature than might have been suspected in the immediate aftermath of Scotland's Union with England in 1707.

In the Glasgow *Bulletin*, 17 January 1921, the poet William Jeffrey published a positive review of C.M. Grieve's anthology *Northern Numbers: First Series* entitled 'Is this a Scottish poetry renaissance?' and

Grieve himself stated boldly: 'the next decade or two will see a Scottish Renascence' in his own magazine, *The Scottish Chapbook*, in August 1922. The French scholar Denis Saurat picked this up in an article entitled 'Le Group de "la Renaissance Ecossaise"' in the *Revue Anglo-Americaine* in April 1924.

Patrick Geddes had held the Chair of Botany at University College Dundee, from 1888 to 1919. After the First World War, he went to India to occupy the Chair of Sociology at the University of Bombay from 1919 to 1924. In 1925, he was back in Scotland, chairing and introducing what was perhaps the first public reading MacDiarmid gave, from his first book of poems, *Sangschaw*, in October 1925, at Ramsay Gardens beside the Outlook Tower at the top of the Royal Mile, just below Edinburgh Castle. At this event, the composer Francis George Scott played his piano settings of some of MacDiarmid's poems. When Chris Grieve was a wee boy in Langholm, Scott had been his English teacher. Now, after the War, they had reconnected in a major ambitious drive towards artistic recovery. MacDiarmid later recollected that when he'd been at school, Scott had administered corporal punishment on at least one occasion. He said he could not remember what he'd done but he was certain he would have deserved it. He and all his classmates were undoubtedly delinquents, he said, and Langholm was a wild and woolly place to grow up in.

So precisely the kind of 'Renascence' that Geddes had envisaged in 1895 was being initiated thirty years later, at this meeting in 1925. The point is that the First World War, the Easter Rising in Ireland and the Russian Revolution had forced it through. These bloody upheavals had forced populations to reconsider what they were fighting for and made possible a new vision from the dead ground of their devastations. According to Geddes's son Arthur, Patrick and he had read MacDiarmid's poems in their home in Montpellier, France, in the French literary periodical *Les Nouvelles Littéraires* (which began publishing in 1922), and Patrick had written to MacDiarmid to introduce himself: hence the meeting.

On 19 October, shortly after the reading and recital, Geddes wrote to Grieve: 'More & more there is growing on me the possibility of strengthening all our scattered movements of synthetic & constructive &

progressive character – whether regional, literary, scientific, artistic, economic or social etc., by trying to bring them together, & thus increasingly present them as each part of a synthetic movement, reaching out beyond the chaos-Babel of current action & thought so apparently predominant.'

In his autobiographical book of essays, *The Company I've Kept,* MacDiarmid wrote: 'This reawakening of the vital and the organic in every department undermines the authority of the purely mechanical. Geddes's prime significance lies in the fact that he was one of the greatest prophets and pioneers of this change.'

For his part, F.G. Scott was a mentor, hard critic, friend and supporter of MacDiarmid and along with Scott's cousin, the artist William Johnstone, the three men saw themselves as the core of the Renaissance movement, in music, poetry and the visual arts. The idea that a cultural and political national rejuvenation in all the arts was underway, moving in every direction, was essential.

It was not an easy road. In an essay from 1925, MacDiarmid says that the Scottish Renaissance is already over – it's happened, done, been and gone – but not gone: 'A certain type of critic is apt to say that the movement consisted only of propaganda – only "of the posters" – that the actual work has still to be done. This is a mistake. The Scottish Renaissance has taken place. The fruits will appear in due course. Earlier or later – that does not alter the fact. For the Scottish Renaissance has been a propaganda of ideas, and their enunciation has been all that was necessary.'

MacDiarmid had seen death at close quarters in the First World War. He had returned from that war with a vision of what a better world might be. And he had a strategy for making Scotland part of it. He wrote and published poetry, journalism, essays, polemics, voluminously. But he made so many enemies among the establishment that by the end of the 1920s he was virtually unemployable. Things were looking desperate. His first wife, Peggy, had had enough. She left him, and took their children with her. All his books went too. He was devastated, went to work in London, was drinking heavily, blundering, trying to keep steady but failing, and then, in Hennekey's bar, High Holborn, he met a young red-haired Cornishwoman named Valda Trevlyn.

A friend, Helen Burness Cruickshank, one of the central enabling figures in modern Scottish literary history, had been in touch with a doctor, David Orr, resident on Whalsay, one of the smaller Shetland islands, and there was the possibility that Valda might find work as a housekeeper for him. Grieve, MacDiarmid, would accompany her there. Since it was a dry island, his friends, and Valda more than anyone, determined that it might be the move to save his life. The gamble was there. The risk.

In 1933, now with Valda his second wife and their young son Michael, he relocated to Whalsay, and they spent most of the next decade in extreme poverty there, in a bare stone house to which water had to be brought up from a well at the bottom of a field sloping down from the back door. I've been there. The well was covered over but my guide and I uncovered it and I leant over, gently brushed away a thin layer of green slime and saw the water, clear and pure. I cupped my hands and took a drink and looked up. Every day, carrying buckets of water from this well, up to that house, one bucket for drinking and cooking, one for washing clothes and bodies. And I turned to look at the sea and the islands all around. And I listened to the water running over the serrated landscapes.

MacDiarmid went out with the fishermen on their boats, 'in line with the Ramna Stacks'. He loved their rough company, their language, their smoking, the strong tea, the stinking socks. Much of his life in Shetland was spent under physical and mental strain, and he went through a physical and mental breakdown and was hospitalised in Perth for months in 1935. But he produced some of his greatest poetry in what he called this 'halophilous living by these far northern seas' (a halophile being a creature that only survives in an atmosphere of salt). Valda saved his life.

The Brownsbank Years

After returning to mainland Scotland in 1941, conscripted into National Service, MacDiarmid spent years at various impermanent homes, mainly in Glasgow, through and after the Second World War. In a 1942 collection entitled *The New Scotland: 17 Chapters on Scottish Reconstruction*, MacDiarmid warmly hailed the appearance of Sorley MacLean, George Campbell Hay, W.S. Graham and others.

At the end of his essay, 'Scottish Arts and Letters: The Present Position and Post-War Prospects' MacDiarmid says this (and the bold at the end is in the original text): 'The [Second World] war may thus have acted as a forcing-bed, bringing to somewhat speedier development what was already securely rooted in the circumstances of our nation; and in this sense it may, perhaps, be said later that: **"The Scottish renaissance was conceived in the First World War, and sprang into lusty life in the Second World War."**'

In 1951, Chris and Valda were given occupancy of the cottage of Brownsbank, just outside Biggar, rent-free, by the benevolent farming family who owned it, the Tweedies. It was an act of great generosity, and that family has an honoured place in Scottish culture's modern history. In this cottage, they were to live together until MacDiarmid's death in 1978, and Valda alone until her own death, in 1989.

When Chris and Valda arrived at Brownsbank in January 1951, it was a hard, cold, snowy winter. The cottage itself was a saviour. There was no indoor toilet as yet, and no running water, but later, in 1967, Valda wrote in a letter to Christopher, 'You know very well – we can manage quite well – we have everything we want'. After decades of poverty and cold, having suffered the indifference and often the outright hostility of the establishment, they had some security at last.

Some critics have suggested that MacDiarmid's best work was over and done with by the time they moved to Brownsbank, that the early lyrics and the poems of the 1920s, and the challenging, philosophical and political poetry of the 1930s, had exhausted his reserves. Not so. In the haven of Brownsbank cottage, the shelter of a home became a cradle for an ever-widening engagement with the changing world, an ever-extending mind enquiring curiously, still challenging the status quo, fighting all the while for a better social structure, and for Scotland's independence. His story was very far from over. What made all this possible was Valda. Valda once wrote: 'We both made sacrifices ourselves. Christopher sacrificed himself – for his principles & I sacrificed myself for Christopher'. It was a sacrifice she made with decision, and she was not a woman to argue with lightly.

In 1952, MacDiarmid published two small books: *Cunninghame Graham: A Centenary Study* and *Francis George Scott: An Essay on the Occasion of his Seventy-fifth Birthday.* His salutation to Cunninghame Graham (1852-1936) takes us back to the foundation of the Labour Party out of the Scottish Labour Party, the Independent Labour Party and the Labour Movement more generally, arising at the end of the 19th century. At that time, the Liberal Party was the only major opposition to the Conservative Party, and all that they stood for: class privilege, inherited wealth, colonial exploitation and imperialism. And it takes us back to the foundation of the National Party of Scotland and the Scottish National Party. Cunninghame Graham spoke out about the need for a socialist future and an independent Scotland to work together to realise the necessary vision. That vision included women's suffrage, Irish reunification, the abolition of the House of Lords and full establishment workers' rights. MacDiarmid said that he dedicated himself to the cause of Scotland, and to opposition to the extraordinary case of Scotland's self-suppression, from the moment he first met Cunninghame Graham.

His tribute to F.G. Scott (1880-1958) takes us back to the intensity of cultural work, the work of the composer and teacher, whose example brought the folk tunes and tones of Scotland and the modernity of Schoenberg and Bartók into new configurations. Scott's was lonely, solitary, dedicated work. He had been an inspiration not only because of his achievement and insight but also because of his integrity. In the 1920s, Scott's settings of MacDiarmid's poems to piano accompaniment were astonishingly modern yet beautifully lyrical, terse yet eloquent, by turns ghostly and mysterious or lovingly poised, rising from profound affirmation. As we noted above, in 1925, in Edinburgh, Scott had performed these songs while MacDiarmid read these early poems at a public occasion presided over by Patrick Geddes. MacDiarmid's tribute to Scott in 1952 was a confirmation of these historical, intellectual and artistic priorities over the decades, and in fact, bridging the centuries across two world wars and connecting his own work, through that of Scott and Geddes, to Allan Ramsay and beyond him, William Dunbar, whose poems Scott also dexterously set to musical accompaniment.

These two slim publications connect the artistic, cultural and political priorities that MacDiarmid held most high. Such priorities remain with us in the 21st century.

In 1955, MacDiarmid published *In Memoriam James Joyce*, the major work of the era, a book-length poem with 'decorations' by the great Scottish artist John Duncan Fergusson. This was MacDiarmid's 'Vision of World Language', an ever-expanding deployment of richly suggestive lists, colourful, provocative, an epic invitation to encounter and explore the work of all the writers and artists he could think of, all the arts and languages and creative compositions of all kinds he could refer to, from all the nations of all the world, throughout history. It is as if he's saying, 'Come on, pilgrims! It's a big world out there – take a big bite!' T.S. Eliot described it as 'a fitting tribute to Joyce' in its magnitude and the sheer variety of its detail.

It is an epic poem whose hero is language – language as both speech and writing, that is, as both musical sound and visual inscription. Its priority is the information and evidence it presents. It does not provide scholarly annotations of the sources from which it was drawn. Most of the lines of the poem come from essays, books and articles written by others but the work's poetic arrangement, whether in subtle lineation and poetic design or in large blocks of data, literary, scientific, biological, speculative or assertive, accumulates to a wholly original achievement, marked by its own character of potentially endless accretion and the inherent possibility of further variations. This epic scale makes it not only a monumental work but a living embodiment in text of the principle of creation from the material reality around us and that runs through us. The whole work speaks of the pathos of the epic effort.

In 1962, at the Edinburgh Festival, he presided over the presentation to Dmitri Shostakovich of Ronald Stevenson's *Passacaglia on DSCH* for solo piano, another epic work, purely musical but packed with references and evocations of cultures, languages, conflicts and tranquilities, the state of the world around him. MacDiarmid's pleasure in bringing Stevenson and Shostakovich together was partly in the recognition of the *Passacaglia*'s realisation of its own 'vision of world language'. There is a complexity in Sandy Moffat's triple portrait of MacDiarmid alongside Stevenson and Shostakovich. Sandy commented: 'Stevenson, Shostakovich and MacDiarmid were communists of sorts, but pre-eminently artists, and for all their sensitivity to the liabilities of the primacy of politics and their commitment to their art, the idealism, or what you might call the pragmatic idealism, their sense of the reality of politics, was interwoven with their commitment to a better social structure and better conditions for people, the destruction of the class system, the hierarchies of privilege. Ronald saw the fall of Communism, and he was a pacifist, deeply committed to the ideal of world peace and a global understanding of the value of peace, and that aligns him with Shostakovich and MacDiarmid particularly in the sense that they were all simultaneously epic artists, and brilliant miniaturists, and they were educationalists, committed to the work of teaching in one way or another. The education of people was a constant and essential priority for all of them.'

Also in 1962, MacDiarmid was visited at Brownsbank by the Russian poet Yevgeny Yevtushenko and the two read together at Glasgow University. And his first *Collected Poems* was published in America. His achievement was beginning to be consolidated and appreciated by a new generation internationally.

The complexity of his position shouldn't be underestimated. Moffat's painting *Milne's Bar* – a complement, perhaps a corrective, to his earlier *Poets' Pub*, presents MacDiarmid beside Valda, with Norman MacCaig placed centrally. Also beside them is Margaret Tait, the poet and film-maker, with her 16mm cine-camera, who, as we mentioned above, made an extraordinary film-portrait of MacDiarmid in 1964. Tait wrote in a letter to Alex Pirie in March 1962, describing her visit to Brownsbank with the photographer Michael Peto when Yevtushenko was there with his girlfriend. Tait tells us: 'The Russians were very fine, very remarkable' but she noted 'MacDiarmid saying quite a lot of rubbish. The Russians bewildered by some of his party line point of view, very far from their own way of expressing themselves. Well, not party line exactly but politically-framed opinions...' MacDiarmid decried the fascist inclinations of T.S. Eliot and Yeats and Valda was sporting a CND 'Ban the Bomb' badge but their Russian visitors seemed puzzled, despite having a good English interpreter with them. Tait observes a kind of mismatch.

Margaret Tait herself was a distinctive poet whose work MacDiarmid published in his magazine *The Voice of Scotland*. Nine of Tait's poems were in proof for the last issue, volume IX, no.3 which was scheduled for 1958-59 but was never printed. The third of these poems is worth quoting here, 'Nothing is Apart':

> Men have wanted poetry to be something apart
> And women to be apart, for them,
> But themselves for women to be 'whole existence.'
>
> What a piece of nonsense!
> Everything is part of whole existence.
> Nothing is apart.

It's almost as if Tait is commenting on the era of the patriarchy which MacDiarmid lived through and to that extent embodied, like so many of his contemporaries and many who preceded and followed from him. And yet, the fact that MacDiarmid championed her work and published it, and was set to publish this poem, suggests that he was aware of the contradictions in which he was immersed, and which he was coming through.

In 1963, MacDiarmid published his translation of Harry Martinson's epic science-fiction poem *Aniara*, a tragic vision of mankind in a post-apocalyptic future. All surviving human beings are leaving the exhausted earth in a spaceship bound for eternal devastation, with only their memories of earth to sustain them. In this terrible scenario, those memories come back to remind the characters – and us, their readers – of why the earth is so valuable, so much to be treasured and why it needs to be looked after carefully.

It's important to remember that MacDiarmid lived across the initiation of the nuclear age. He had seen the rise of fascism in Spain from 1936 and wrote passionately denouncing the supporters of the dictator Franco; he had witnessed the horrors of the Second World War, not only the physical devastations but the growing degradations of propaganda. This was evident to him not just in the rise of Nazism but in mass media techniques of persuasion, and their extensive application in the west through the Cold War, which led straight to 21st-century populism. And he was keenly aware that the romantic ideal that the resources of earth are infinitely renewable was ended: after 1945, they could be destroyed by humankind. His translation of *Aniara* is his testament to this.

In 1964, he engaged with Hamish Henderson in a flyting in the letters pages of *The Scotsman* – a public argument of extreme verbal flair and uninhibited opposition, clashing on the matter of the value of 'folk song' as opposed to 'high art' and classical music. On 7 March, MacDiarmid wrote: 'The demand everywhere today is for higher intellectual levels. Why should we be concerned then with songs which reflect the educational limitations, the narrow lives, the poor literary abilities, of a peasantry we have happily outgrown?' Henderson's response was vigorous: 'Mr MacDiarmid displays not the smallest comprehension of the difference between traditional song-poetry in the folk idiom and the lucubrations of minor or minimal scribblers who in every age are the dim also-rans of "art poetry".'

And MacDiarmid replied in kind: 'At the present stage in human history, there are far more important things to do than bawl out folksongs…' Henderson insisted on the value of 'the continuing vitality' of the folk tradition, and that 'To oppose creative art to folk "interpretation" is a false dichotomy.'

This was an explosive exploration of polarities, with 'working-class' and 'bourgeois' representatives. In a world so controlled by authorities who sought to foster divisiveness, who knew the benefits of fragmentation, MacDiarmid and Henderson set out to explore the extremes, and see just how far the arguments could go. The bringing back together of these extremes – their meeting – is enacted in Moffat's painting *Scotland's Voices*.

In fact, eleven years before this flyting, MacDiarmid had firmly endorsed the virtues of the folk tradition in an essay entitled 'To Hell with Culture' (1953): 'I have known Edinburgh intimately for nearly half-a-century, and I could count the cultured Edinburgh citizens I have met in it on fewer than the fingers of one hand. Most of them are dead now.' Nevertheless, he goes on: 'I did meet certain really cultured people at the Festival time last year – at a concert that wasn't on the official Festival programme. It was a ceilidh at which the programme was sustained by Gaelic and Lallans folk-singers. There was a young boy from Turriff who sang like a lintie songs that had been orally transmitted for generations in his family. There was an old farm-wife of over 70. There was a tramp singer who had been travelling the roads of Scotland all his days.'

He concludes: 'It was one of the finest concerts I ever attended. *The Scotsman* and all the other papers didn't print a word about it. These Scottish folk-singers were real artists. Every one of them was culturally worth all the famous artistes, conductors, actors and actresses of the official festival a thousand times over. These folk-singers will never be decorated or named to an academy. When their voices fail they will probably starve to death. But whenever you hear one of them singing you have there before you the aesthetic impulse of all times (genuine even if often on a merely elementary level) – and another exemplification of the way in which in Scotland we have bartered our birthright for a mess of commercialised cosmopolitan pottage.'

This polemic comes from a depth of experience of poverty, and of taking the social risk of integrity standing against an ethos of utter venality, and from a profound understanding of cultural value, internationally and historically. That, too, is MacDiarmid's example. His contradictions are most frequently not an act of irresponsibility but rather an expression of his dedication and an exemplification of his energy.

Plurality is the answer, within the archipelagic and land-based territories, the haunted seas and landscapes of an independent Scotland, where the values of diversity, difference, opposition and affirmation cannot be dissolved. Geography and language are our only defining factors. MacDiarmid shows us how the arguments have to be occupied, exercised and gone through before full recognition of the way so many different perspectives can inform each other gainfully. Thus the composers Janáček, Bartók, F.G. Scott and Erik Chisholm might all come into a new configuration. Traditional music and song, so often composed and performed by women, form the strengths and heart in F.G. Scott's solo piano pieces *Intuitions*, as well as in his settings of MacDiarmid, Burns, William Dunbar and other poets. This is the true meaning of 'popular': not commercially exploitative but '*di essenza popolare*' – of the people.

In June 1973, MacDiarmid read alongside Allen Ginsberg at the Rotterdam International Poetry Festival, and Ginsberg visited Chris and Valda at Brownsbank, sharing a smile and a sunny conversation. Valda once spoke to me of how he'd brought some 'interesting tobacco' with him and offered to share it around. Valda was eager to participate. Chris held shy of that, preferring his own malt whisky. Ginsberg went on to Iona, writing in the poem 'Mind Breaths' (dated September 28, 1973): 'over Iona blue day and balmy Inner Hebridean breeze, fog drifts across the Atlantic': Scotland was a necessary part of his journey too.

Near the end of his long life, in 1978, MacDiarmid was visited by the young artist Sandy Moffat, who began to sketch his portrait, with a sense of urgency, knowing that this was to be an essential record of a great poet, his image captured in art on the very edge of his life. Just as MacDiarmid had lived 'where extremes meet', the artist and the poet were meeting at a crossroads in both their lives.

MacDiarmid saw the proofs of his two-volume *Complete Poems* before he died on 9 September, at the age of 86. He knew he had done as much as he could. His son Michael Grieve wrote of his father's last days in Chalmers Hospital, in Edinburgh: 'At the very end, in the evening of his last night and unable to speak, though his eyes were still glowing with understanding and intelligence, he turned his head to the window and looked out to the Edinburgh skyline. A little later Scotland seemed "a colder and quieter place".'

He could not have seen in that Edinburgh landscape what we see there now, a new parliament, a building in which we have our own government. On the walls of that parliament are quotations from a range of Scottish poets, in the three major languages – Gaelic, Scots and English – in which our literature has been composed over centuries.

He could not have foreseen these things but he would have been as fierce a critic of their limitations as of their opponents, those who would foreclose the parliament, the government and the entire national culture of which they are an expression. The fact that such opposition exists and has not ceased to be active is what his legacy was made to resist.

Prospects

The threats that MacDiarmid lived through – two world wars, the rise of fascism in Spain in the 1930s, the Cold War – predate those of the 21st century, the impending catastrophes of climate and global ecology, the sweeping contagions of disease and the corruptions of the ideals of human agency that are developed in particular forms in every era. But what gave rise to them has never really gone away and he can still show us ways to resist them. We shall need these methods and examples for it seems that now as then our languages, Gaelic and Scots, our entire cultural history and its living practice in education and social engagement, in all the difficulties and pleasures art can bring, that which gives us human learning, must be fought for once again. The battle continues.

When Alexander Moffat first sketched Chris Grieve in 1978, and when I first met him in 1977, none of us could have foreseen the achievements and the threats that were to come. The last time I met him, near the end of his life, I asked with the fury of youth, 'When?'

MacDiarmid raised his eyebrows. Chris, he said I should call him. That wasn't quite right. And 'Dr Grieve' was too formal. I think I remember that I called him Christopher. 'You've called for all these things, and argued, written so much, so passionately, Scotland's independence, socialism, a better place to live in, the well-being of people, all these things, *when* do you think it might happen?'

He smiled and nursed his pipe, puffed, and said, 'Alan, when you get to my age, the urgency is less important.'

Which is why the young, generations to come, need to know. I hope that the poems in this book, alongside Sandy's paintings of the poet and his wife and friends, and Ruth's paintings of his landscapes, might return us to the whole trajectory of his life, the world that surrounded him, geographical, historical, and political.

The poems might not all explain themselves at first, entirely. There is no quick fix here. But maybe the curious will find something to be hooked by, happily. In a society like ours, that's as good a start as any.

Here are the Borders, the rivers he listened to as a boy, here is Montrose, centre of the Scottish Renaissance in the 1920s, here are the islands of Shetland, here is a diverse geography enduring through a history of revolutionary change and here, finally, is the old man himself, glass in hand, seated in his Brownsbank armchair, slippers on for comfort, but suited, sharp, and looking up and out at you. Perhaps he is asking us all:

What do you want, you who are alive now, looking at me, here, today? Read my work and ask yourselves, what do you want for the future?

Alan Riach, 2023

The MacDiarmid Memorandum

Discretions

'My life has been an adventure, or series of adventures, in the exploration of the mystery of Scotland's self-suppression.'
– Hugh MacDiarmid, *Lucky Poet* (1943)

'A recent writer said it isn't surprising that so many people who have got used to this society resist deep analysis of its forms. The forms of accepted analysis, and the judgements that go with them, are part of the deep accommodation to an orthodox consciousness.'
– Hugh MacDiarmid, 'Scotland: Full Circle' (1971)

'A poet's work [is] to name the unnameable, to point at frauds, to take sides, start arguments, shape the world and stop it from going to sleep.'
– Salman Rushdie, *The Satanic Verses* (1988)

'From one crucible of the imagination, alchemists of the temper of a Lovelace, George Lamming, Chinua Achebe, Charles Dickens, Tolstoy, Emile Zola, wa Thiongo, Camara Laye, Banumbir Wongar…from yet another, Garcia Marquez, Amos Tutuola, Verlaine, Rimbaud, Genet, and again Banumbir Wongar and Camara Laye… fundamentally one material world, one physical reality. Yet, in different degrees, our sorcerers construct and communicate wildly separated yet coherent structures of a new reality, implying a refusal to accept that the empirical dictum of reality is all there is – or else, why write?'
– Wole Soyinka, 'New Frontiers for Old' (1990)

'There's an invisible presence in this room, whom I want to invoke: the great Scottish Marxist bard Hugh MacDiarmid. I'll begin by reading from his exuberant, discursive manifesto called, bluntly, *The Kind of Poetry I Want*. [This is a] manifesto of desire for "a new and conscious organisation of society" and a poetic view to match it. A manifesto that acknowledges the scope, tensions, and contradictions of the poet's undertaking. Let's bear in mind the phrases "difficult knowledge", "the concentrated strength of all our being", the poem as "wide-angled" but also the image of the poet as nurse in the operating theatre: "fully alert". [...] There is always (I am quoting the poet/translator Américo Ferrari) "an unspeakable where, perhaps, the nucleus of the living relation between the poem and the world resides." The living relation between the poem and the world: difficult knowledge, an operating theatre where the poet, committed, goes on working.'

– Adrienne Rich, 'Poetry & Commitment' (2006)

Thir ar the dayes that thou sa lang foretald
Sould cum befoir this wretchit warld sould ende.
Now vice abounds and charitie growes cald,
And evin thine owne most stronglie dois offend –
Thocht Tirannes freat, thocht Lyouns rage & roir,
Defy them all and feir not to win out –

– Elizabeth Melville, *Ane Godlie Dreame* (1603)

The road of excess leads to the palace of wisdom.

– William Blake, *The Marriage of Heaven and Hell* (1790-93)

A Border Boyhood

Three Rivers

        Langholm, at the confluence –
            of the Wauchope, the Esk and the Ewes –
Listen like a blind man, let the sounds go in,
            ears open to the cradle of
                that territorial cusp
        And scents: the honey-fragrant heather hills,
    a world made of borders, all around –
The hard one
    To the south, to be held.
        The differentiations, fierce,
            the echo effects, close,
                the gurgle and the gargle of
Running water, riverbeds and stream curves,
            currents and banks, the trees and forests above
    The flagstones, rocks and bridges,
        factory walls and windows soaking up the watery reflections –
The waterside folk, the folk in the town, those on the hill,
                    under the shade of the trees –
The four hills of Whita, Warblaw, Meikleholm with its Tinpin knoll, the Castle
    The valleys cut and carved by liquid nourishment, replenishment –
Eight miles away, the English,
        and once a year, in touching distance, there,
    From Square to hillside, hilltop, marches all around,
        early, first, the dogs,
    The racing baying hounds, and then,
        the morning horses in the Square:
From stand and snort and stable, to the Crying of the Fair
And then the stout command!
    And gallop.
        Inches from your touch,
                hundreds of galloping horses, riders
    Keen and ruddy, thighs and boots,
        belted, braced and helmeted, eyes
Forward for the summit and the curving tracks and trails that mark
A territory guarded by inhabitants,
        the folk who live there now.

The learning

All things bright and beautiful, all creatures,
Great and small,
All rainbows' colours, storms and showers,
All things that rise and fall –
Stones and mountains, rivers, seas, and oceans far between,
Heather moors and hillsides, squat bushes, trees so tall –
The languages we use and are, to say that's there, to point,
Or else to tell us who we are, the call
Of others, company, communities of selves,
And differences marked between, what voices are, and all
Such annotations, permutations, collocations mean
Is what we learn from womb to coffin's floor and wall
Of earth or water, fire or air, we give what bodies as we have,
Surrender them, at last. This ball
Of earth, the sphere, the globe, the knowledge thus acquired
Is what's forever, always here, evolving into what's desired,
And taking forms to do so, in an age of revolutions.
So many kinds of learning are the only real solutions.
Resolve and resolutions, complexities, collusions,
Relax: and we achieve what comes, inevitable life. We're stuck
With it, for that's what learning is. It comes to us, with luck.

The Purchase of Tarras Moor

And what can this place be?
High moor and wiry bush, Bolshevik bog, vast field of
Utter self-possession. What can purchase mean
In such a place of desolation? No. Not
Desolation. Simply something live beyond the human,
For contrast, think: The gentleness of grass,
Soft green, and neatly mown, but tall enough
To welcome little hands and cheeks to touch its yielding
Blades. As when our young son James, an infant,
Rolled from the woollen travelling rug,
Cunningham tartan, black and red,
As Rae and I were setting things upon it for the picnic,
All in the green grass yard, surrounded by the ruined walls
Of tall Dunnottar Castle, in the far north-east, and James
Discovers grass, for the first time, only once,
Can such a touch be made. Surprise and wonder,
Sensual engagement. We paused to look at him, his
Wee boy's curiosity and intimate attachment, seeing,
Touching, this material thing, he'd never been so close to,
In his life. But Tarras Moor? Another world.
A place that only those possessed by it, possess.
The ownership was then but now no longer
The estate of the Duke of Buccleuch. What purpose he delivered,
Making certain through whatever needful economic structures
Organised the sale, the whole thing went in one, the right,
Direction? But more, what strength, determination, vast intense
And purpose-driven gathering of cash resources led
That group of common people bound together
To take the first initiative, to buy the land, to win
The land, and not for them, but for all folk to come,
And not for them, but all the beasts and insects,
Birds and fish and reptiles, all the wiry bushes and the trees,
Both tall and stunted, in its grand expanse of wilderness,
The clouded air above it and the rain?
An effort of the will of a collective, made reality
Present. A gift. The only true investment: land,
The water, earth. Hugh MacDiarmid walked this moor,
A hundred years ago, or more. The wet came through to his feet.
His fingers and nails dug into the dirt. He breathed the scent
Of its mosses. Just as our James was buoyant on the grass,
This dark elation came with intimate association, firmly
Lodged within imagination, words, and breath, and touch.
That's purchase, he to it and it to him, forever,
As now, to us.

The Library

This is what brainwashing means:
A laundry basket full of books.

And if there were twelve thousand books,
And if he'd read them all before he left, at age sixteen,

And if he started reading aged, say, eight,
He would have had to read at least four books a day

For every day for every single one
Of those eight years.

Which is not impossible,
I guess.

But still quite hard
To credit.

The Ministry of Water

It's water, not the fish, that needs attention.
Others might angle, and losing the catch, jump in,
Into the river, splashing for the thing –
No – the thing is now and always has been, will be still in time to come –
To see: to love the water for colour and sound and movement,
A thoosan' things that ithers never see: The light in twirls and bobs,
Shades and taints, tinges and timbres and tones, queer wee cracks and bubbles,
Croichles, blawps and blares, and soothes of grooves and runnelings –
Crochet-patterns in the foam, intricate lacings and tracings –
All lost in the general roar, all buried in the moss of grasp and greed,
All dead to a world so wrapped up and swamped in motivation,
Misplaced, mistaken, slipped from any sense
Within the soaring human yabble-yabble.
Be motiveless. Be still. Be the observant eye.

The Border Guards

There were three on the line, each one skilled
By their vision, how their minds fashioned
Construction. Thus, the shape of their skulls, the placement
Of eyes, the muscles that lifted their cheeks when they smiled,
The angle of neck, the movement of muscle and bone,
Extending into torso, arms and hands and fingers, finger-tips on keys,
Long wooden-handled brushes, rags and canvases,
Pens and pencils, paper, wooden easels, desks or tables,
The place of writing, painting, composition, transference
Of what breathed in might then be formed in notes, in shapes of colour
And in words.
               Three on the line, defending the border.
March men, riders on skyline and river valley, tracing the contours of hills,
The edges of the territories, wilderness made form, energy
In shapes.
        This is where the line was drawn and set.
This was how transgression was defined: multiple,
Vertical, sheer. Not linear, uncrossable, closed. But high,
And interpenetrative. Two were cousins. All were friends,
And teachers. They learned each others' methods of perception,
Which helped them differentiate their own.
They came to understand how art's participation
Is only in the act of making actual, the practice of the balancing
Material, and what immaterial is, reality's creation, and learned
That that is always what's at stake. The mortal cost is permanent,
And always present tense. Abstractions were what each of them
Would know, but yet, the tensile strengths of artefacts,
In music, painting, poetry and writing in a multitude of manners,
Made things, the works of art, are at the furthest place
From such abstractions.
                      And so are the abstractions.
William Johnstone's lithographs define,
Like nothing else, what textures are, what ink can do on paper,
Where the limits of articulation are, the borders.
They come from understanding landscapes, people's faces
As the landscapes of the world. F.G.'s songs are momentary, intuitions,
Justified and self-sustained by the quickness of the edges rising
Out of human depths. MacDiarmid's poems in this place
Like a handful of bones on the cave floor, thrown,
Telling the truth to those who can read. A scattering

Of meaningless calcium, lines dried out, a mere pretence,
To anyone else. Only them as can see, maybe can see what they saw.
We'll see.
    Let's take them in their turn, and then
Together, as they were, a partnership of spikes,
A trinity of inequalities, facing with arms extended,
Palms open, outstretched, reaching towards different points,
The craftsman's tools, the implements, the armoury of peace,
Making a network of ley lines, an
Invisible cradle of cables, electrified
By art, good humour, and
What self-determination comes to be.

The Scottish Soul

'The problems o' the Scottish soul
Are nocht to Harry Lauder…'

So what did this atheist mean by 'soul'?
What but that corporeal thing, the spirit, singular
To each identity, collectively shared by all,
Across the earth, and through all time,
Struggling into being:
Given, lent, undefined and unfulfilled,
Forgiven, lost, and unrecorded. Human and all other
Potential. What dominates all his poetry and prose
Is this complete conviction: 'that all accepted belief –
All social, religious, and legal conviction – is sham,
That only anguished confrontation, with the absurd,
Can free the soul from that worse fate of blind hypocrisy –
From the oppression of received opinion
And a sheer timidity of mind.'

World War I: Empires & small nations

'It took the full force of the war to jolt an adequate majority of the Scottish people out of their old mental, moral and material ruts… The Scottish Renaissance movement regards itself as an effort in every respect of the national life to supplant the elements at present predominant by the other elements they have suppressed, and thus reverse the existing order.'

– Hugh MacDiarmid (1927)

Cultural Appropriation

The Black & White Minstrel Show is cultural appropriation.
Karl Marx writing for the working class is representation.
Harry Lauder's Canny Scotsman is cultural appropriation.
Charlie Chaplin's Little Tramp represents the dignity
And sympathy of working people.
And their resourcefulness and humour. And their desperation.

There are differences.

Then there are the Apologists.
The Black & White Minstrel Show is a fact of Music Hall history.
And Harry Lauder was very popular throughout the world.
And after all he lost a son in the First World War,
Raised money for the troops, and charity.
We should celebrate our Music Hall history
And not be such cultural elitists!

The First World War was made
By Lauder's propaganda
(That's called synecdoche)
What comes out of it, and what came before it.
Just as the *Black & White Minstrel Show*
Came straight out of slavery
And slavery has never really gone away,
One way or another.
And as surely as our leaders have killed by buffoonery,
Enslaved and grown richer by methods,
As they puff out their cheeks through their collars of ermine,
Pontificate out of their mantles of lordliness,
Lauder, like all of them, pockets the cash.
He carries more guilt than his fortunes could cushion him from.
Don't ask me to find him funny as well.

Such royalty of Music Hall and Cinema,
And the gold-embrazened carriage on the Mall,
Their pageantry & pomp –
Oh, horrible crowds!
Just throw yourselves before them,
With all the self-debasement you can muster.
And let it all run over you
Like tanks at Cambrai.

Europe's far enough for me

In the near and middle distance, the destruction,
Boots and puttees, khaki: up to ankles, mud, and up to knees,
At times, in water, puddles, ordure, stench
Of blood and body parts and bits of men, the flesh and bones,
The remnants of the carcasses of empire.
To think what mind can do: the reading, plans
For writing. Afterwards, the trauma: 'Never again
Must men endure such things'. And if 'for little Belgium's sake',
What of 'little Scotland'? Scotland, small?
That vulnerable place: Scotland, small? Be inside its borders,
Let its scale and depth, diversity, begin to blossom out
Within your vision. Set the sights on this:
Locality, the voices and the languages
Of women and of men, children and the aged: Scots, Gaelic,
English as we have it here, and all that our geography creates.
Beyond that, Europe, far enough, for now.
Beyond that, all the world, archipelagos of furtherance, forever.
There is no end to what we see beginning now.
This battle will continue. This revolution's permanent.

Renaissance

Vortex

At the still centre of the world exploding, centrifugal, centripetal, whirligigs and dead e
Opening out to avenues, the estuary, old Montrose, the sea coast within sight
F.G. and the night of assembly, fragments and freight, balanced, connected and loade
All the ammunition needed for the big push forward, the sweep and cycle, reach and dep
The dark depression of the cat's eyes inward-turning, those reflective, introverted insigh
Perception going inward, through the bone to marrow,
And outward round the globe, that vast inhuman cosmos and its music
The poems soaring rockets of delivery that rises, upwards, still, impossible trajectories
Dead sticks come down to litter the ground, the earth that never really lets us go

Company

Explosive force, imagination's purpose: Johnstone's *Points in Time*, F.G.'s
Intuitions, those defined arpeggios, accompaniments, interpretations,
Love's caress, acknowledgements of contours, shapeliness, forms.
Painting, music, sculpture, dance, plays and angels, ballet, film,
Photography, philosophy, the world of language, language made
By worlds of things and purposes, of drives, of look out where
You're going, drive, regardless, take it forward, headed, one-way,
Always: Crosbie, Carswell, Shepherd, the Muirs, McCance and Lamb,
From Cairncross to Cruickshank, from Ogilvie to Stevenson, and on.

Home

Domestic bliss unbalanced by commitments and temptations: fanatic vision,
Alcohol, a loyalty to letters, country, betterment, to hope, to insecurity,
Uncertainty, to risk. Or else to all that otherwise might offer comfort, safety,
An element of luxury, some respite from the fight. So family and books are gone,
And what remains is strung out, salvaged by rescue from Cornwall, lifted,
Up from the stairwell of Hennekey's, High Holborn, north to a Shetland in distance.

Love & loss

Velvet is too hard a thing
To say, those lips, the parts, the partings, the departing
The vulnerable lips, the body's touch, a kiss,
A rose, that red rose now become
A bloody mess, a tortured turn of flesh and loss,
The loss of all I thought she was –
As women were, the pedestal on which
We placed them, in our gaze – all gone –
And with her gone, the children –
Home, the books –
A world of mind a sense of what I might have once called purity,
My own –
(Knowing even then it was a lie)
But I came out of the nineteenth century –
Oh, no excuse, I know, of course, but try to understand
As I did not, back then, that that's what men were like,
And still, so many of us, are, and that's what women too,
Were like, and still, so many of them, are. What can I do
Now, but stumble into drink and dumb
Obscurity? Unless a hand comes down,
Some gift of fortune, luck entailed –
By whatever effort I might make, some gesture, risk,
A kindness, token, offered, come what may,
This is why we search beyond the self –
Results that you could never have predicted. Nothing
Planned, the bagatelle keeps following, I
Hold my place in its impulsive movement.
The great wheel turns. And I a single note
In some unheard-of symphony. A blade of grass
On a mountain slope, or, no, a single drop of morning dew
Upon it, melts, in sunshine, in the morning.

Prelude to Shetland

Before they went to Shetland,
The family came to Corstorphine
To stay with Helen Cruikshank,
Who had hired a pram for Michael
And the three of them walked out in sunshine,
And the fourth, in a pram,
The poet as 'domestic as a plate'
Pushing the pram and Michael
Up and down the hilly roads,
With Valda by him on one side,
Helen on the other,
Laughing, laughing merrily,
In the high cool air of winter.

MacDiarmid on Whalsay

A Glass of Cold Water, Mid-Afternoon

A house at home in Arctic winds in
the outbreak of war, the North Sea when it was
the German, spike-helmeted, silver and black,
glittering (ever the best in uniform, the Nazi sky
and ocean, inhumanly and humanly unmerciful). And
you're there trying hard, doing what you can to help
the listed poems escape. Weather is one thing,
daily, accumulating change. This is another: this
is the climate. Set yourself against it: the words
lean on the window-panes and rattle their frames
like iron bars; night and the stormtroops lean in.

Air Salt Stone

Benign on the inlets and islets of inside, of
Langerhans, the warm sun shines for a long time
each and every day, on all the 'corrugations' and
the 'coigns'. Each word is a delicate finger-tip's
print tracing gently with pressure on each turning
shape, the stones themselves mere metaphors for
these attempts to charge them with a meaning.
Night earns it, but, day brings it, sometimes. Not
every day. All every day will bring is, mushrooms,
mackerel, washing-up, good water from the well.
But some days like that sunshine, touching, lat-
erally, over all: inside, out, and there, benign.

Valda and Michael

I see her hands and arms, the strengths in bone
and muscle, her fingers round the string run
through the gills of sillocks, her clothes coarse
and warm, her independence, guidance, giving,
glee. Her laughter, lips, her voice. His voice,
His march of childhood, sheer Shetlandic
balance, care, assertiveness, set in a world
where shelter is less frequent and more welcome,
the edge never easy but ubiquitous, the crash and
cry of gulls' flight, waves, time marked, ferries
booming horns away, bells ringing into all the
horizons opening out and closing in, to deadlines.

MacDiarmid on Whalsay

music: Ronald Stevenson August 2004
a setting of a poem by Alan Riach

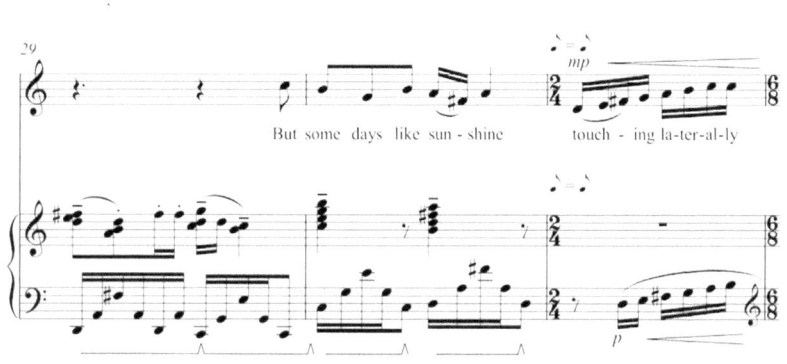

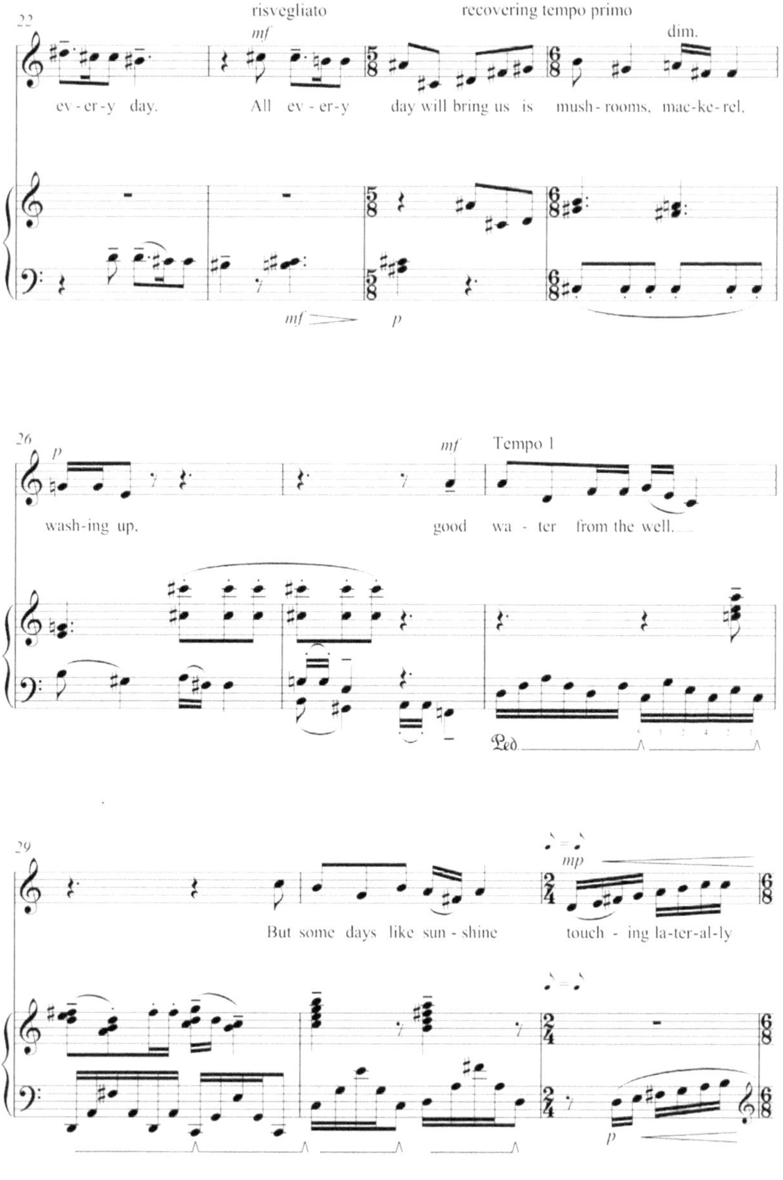
22
risvegliato
recovering tempo primo
mf
dim.
ev - er - y day.
All ev - er - y
day will bring us is
mush - rooms, mac - ke - rel,
mf
p
26
p
mf
Tempo I
wash - ing up,
good
wa - ter
from the well.
Ped.
29
mp
But some days like sun - shine
touch - ing la - ter - al - ly
p

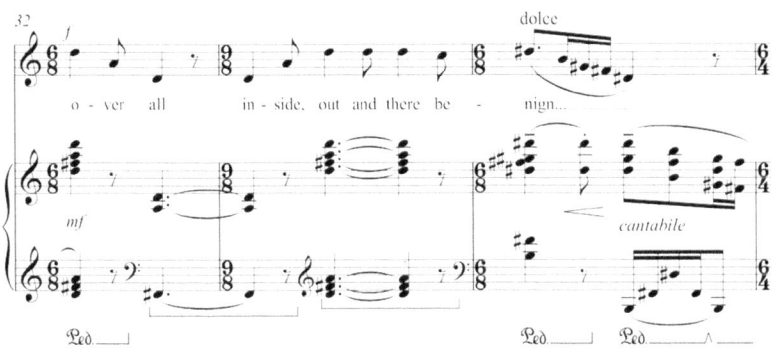
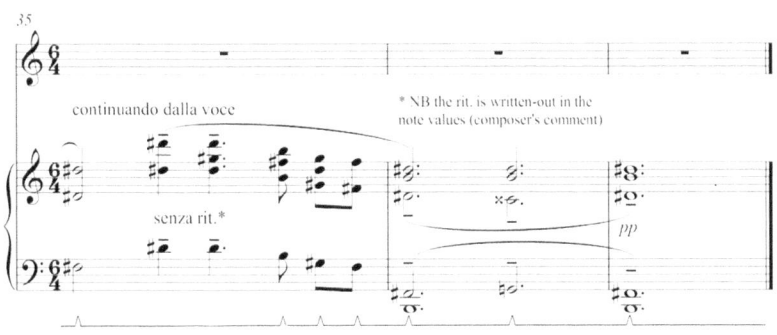

MI5

An 'Enemy of the State'? They got that right, at least.
Why Orwell tipped them off that he'd be most susceptible
To Communism, should it arrive, was so much in plain sight
He must have known, redundant from the start. Why bother?
Why not? 'We have an eye on him,' wrote Monocle McGonigal,
The Captain from Carstairs. 'We'll keep him under observation.'
Before they sent him south to Glasgow, for work in a munitions
Factory, rather than mending the roads. Poor work for a would-be tramp.
'He plays chess with the Laird,' somebody noted. A fine thing to do
For a Commie. 'He jist disny work avaa,' another said.
What work he did, what work we do, what steely weight of purpose, drive
And utter dedication? Valda rushing to rescue the balled-up solid parcel
Of neatly scrawled-on paper hurled with a rage of destruction
Into the flames in the hearth. Sparks everywhere, patting out the flares
At papers' edges, blackened, charred corners, but the poetry still,
Discernible, still readable, still there. Their eyes are on him now. The words remain.

Technique & Ideation

Which is what he said in 1922: To bring Scotland now into closer alignment
With Europe in matters of 'technique and ideation'. 'Technique' is clear enough:
Modernism: Pound, Joyce, Eliot, but also Mayakovsky, Valéry, Verhaeren,
Eluard, Hikmet, and further, later: Neruda, Cardenal, those whom he endorsed, approv
Understood (as far as he needed to): So far, so good, in terms of 'technique'.
But 'ideation'? Well, ideas, certainly, but also perhaps, creation, negotiation, forming,
Formation, in formation, aborning: what was being made, in the aftermath
Of World War One, after the clash of Empires, leading only further,
Towards the bias and thwart and clash again of greater Empires,
Countered by and only by, what poets and artists might do,
And do, have done, will do, in any such singular place as they have,
And in their singular nation. But it goes further still. Not only human forms of word
Of languages, but music, too, the music of the earth, the languages
Of trees and stones, of birds and beasts and oceans, seas, rivers, rain.

With the fishermen

On his back in his bunk with his paper fixed fast
On the slats of the bunk bed above him, his fingers hard pressed
Holding it there, spread flat in front of his face,
While his right hand holding the pencil comes up and the graphite makes marks
As he scribbles and scrawls as the waves toss the boat and the words
Cloud around down the hatchway from them, from their throats,
Through their mouths, from the sailors, on deck,
The fishermen moving and hauling on nets, running them out,
And pulling them in with the silver on board, hoards upon hoards
Of the shoals of the fish and lines upon lines upon page after page,
As the hold fills up and the paper is filled with the words
And the pages are stuffed in his bag by his side by the bunk.
'What's that? What's that word? What's that phrase? What's that mean?'
And he's learning it fast, he scribbles it down. These men know their language,
Devised as it is for their purpose. And he puts their words into his poems.
'What's that? What's he up to? Scribblin' it doon, takkin' the tune
O' oor talkin'?' His eyes flicker up, flick back from the hatch to the paper,
The pencil as it scratches and rolls, as the boat rolls and pitches, drives on
Through the seas, in a line with the stacks,
The rocks that reach up to the tatters of clouds,
As he reaches up with his pencil to pin
The words of the seafarers down on the page.
But then they will seek to outsmart him.
They're making up words, the nonsense of phrases
Bandied between them, and then his brow frowns in perplexity,
Eyebrows in crunched concentration, his pencil is stalled,
The boat's engine splutters and coughs. But then he will outsmart them all.
The words will go into the poems. Actual words, the phrases in use,
And with them the words all made up for invention, for fun, just for mischief.
They all go into the poetry, that's what it's for, its recipient –
In an atmosphere made thick
With smelly socks and black tobacco clouds
Salt air and wet cascades of sea, wood and engine fumes and fish.
The words as elemental and the pencil and the page
And the books they will turn into
And the eyes that come to read them, ages hence.

Onwards

The enemy regroups. Like isolated pools of molten metal,
Finding themselves, connecting and reforming
As in fascicles of force, the broken empires of a First World War
Become a fascist Falange, forcing
Spain into its grinding years and Stalin
Into his, and then the Cold War icing all that heat
Into potential outburst, Merlin's revenge,
And then reforming that, when David turns Goliath
And the rule becomes the government
Of that tripartite law: of Ignorance,
Stupidity, Malevolence: of cowards, fools and monsters:
Of human beings at their worst.
There is no end of needed words
To offer to oppose the like of this.

World War II: Fascism & populism

The lines of men

It's Beckett's line, and the Second World War
Is its cradle. There's death. And there's the witnessing.
And the witness continues to suffer, suffers more.
Beckett was wrong. It's not a fair comparison.
Maybe. It's preferable to suffer than be gone.
Is it? Yes. It is. But what are you choosing?
'So I see the armies of the world once more
As I saw them a quarter of a century ago…'
– There is more pathos in those two lines
Than any further still elaboration. And yet.
'The worst is not yet when we can say,
This is the worst.' The words most hopeful in *King Lear*,
The happiest moment in the play, the words most full of
That despair: of recognition. There is no recovery from this.
The world has turned into something now quite
Irretrievable. Everything else is a dream, a fantasy.
Reality's just this: a cycle of descent, a vortex of the worst
That multiplies the worst and takes us all down with it.
'And I alone survived to tell the tale…'
Well, maybe. Who's to say? And who's to tell the tale to?
The rise of fascist Europe was just the place and time.
'All that's eternal fears fulfilment.' Fine.
What sort of fulfilment would you like?
Here's one. It takes a bit more time. And the pathos is,
You have a chance, humanity. 'The worst is not yet…'
Until the words run out. Until the silence rules.
And even then, it is residual? Don't trust to that.
Exhaustion dictates: rest. Others will come. Don't
Ruin yourself. Survival is priority, and memory, thus: art.

But oh, what despair! What terminal despair to see it all
Happening again. As he saw it all
Happening again, only worse, for two reasons:
One, it was happening again. And two, it was worse, more widespread
And intrinsic to modernity. Everything that's possible breeds
Its own impossibility, and cancellation. Every achievement made
Creates barbaric consequence. And all we struggle for and towards
Prompts a greater force against itself. But then:
Even the deepest things that humankind can do,
Nature will return to correct, a deeper nature, then, intended to correct
What humankind has done, will do, to it, or her, or what its inmost self might be.
We cannot understand.
No consolation there at all. Only the question, first and last,
When it comes to taking sides, which side are you on?

The World Language

'The ideal observer of art at work would be one conscious of all human experience up to given moment. (The ideal observer of art – as against art-at-work – is God, conscious of that has been and will be achieved.)' – Hugh MacDiarmid, 'Art and the Unknown' (192

And of course, it had to be 'from'
'A Vision of World Language'
Because such a vision complete
Could not be comprehended
By anyone or anything,
Except, of course, the invention of 'God'.
No reference exists for: 'God'.
Take that word out and what have you left?
The observer of: A vision of world language:
All the languages of the world, all forms of expression,
In every nation, region, location,
Across millennia, in all their transformations,
Through time, from then and there,
Wherever, whenever, till now.

And more: from now
Across all that's yet to come, and everywhere.
And through all the galaxies even now appearing to our eyes.
So this applies now, to me as I write, to you as you read.
Wherever, whenever you are. You.
All such things in human and inhuman terms
Struggle to find their forms of self-expression,
This struggle is the language of the world,
The vision of 'world language' is thereby thus defined.
A world in the process of always giving birth to itself,
And poets and artists always in the function of
The advocates. They are the defenders, not of faith, but life.
Nurses, doctors, midwives in the theatre of operations.
Because that's what we're out for, not just more, but better.

Cottage

'Now we have all we need' – no drains, no indoor running water,
No toilet, and poverty is as it was, but Valda: now we have all we need:
A roof, two beds, two hearth-fires, rooms to live in, breathe in,
Read in, write in, think – and listen to the opposition,
All those voices coming through in English, radio waves, and
All that screened and screening American trash, junk Scottish pap,
The scum of the universe, magnified and avalanched –
And then the solitary visitors, the mercies enacted
Of great aspirations: Yevtushenko, Ginsberg;
Salutations from admirers: Lowell, Heaney;
Visits to Pound, to Mao, to Ireland and America;
And friends: MacCaig, MacLean and Stevenson;
Family: Michael and Deirdre, grandchildren, close
– And still the world to fight for.

The Seasons

Winter

White winter, ice and snow all over
Everything, the road, though, still, to be discerned,
Traced, tracked, leading us out, welcoming
The visitors, air in the throat, in the lungs,
Cold, ragged, emitted in clouds from the singular
Personal breath, the aural world of frost crunch
Grass bent down in white weight, rustling, all things
Hardened and requiring the resistance of the body,
Its warmth, wrapped up in wool, with only the eyes
As sharp as what they see, what must be seen
And so, preserved, protected, or moved into, changed
Forever into something better. All this landscape
Is the winter mind, filled with the strength of the living,
Balanced on movement and residence, in this endless open air.

Spring and Summer

Sowing time and farmers' fields becoming
Seeded, timed in weeks and months, to turn green
Brown, the earth churned over, ploughed for
The harvest to come. And then long summer's round,
High skies, dwarfing all beneath, balanced by the sheer investment
Such relations make between the human and the flowers and crops,
The trees and bushes, what's protective, what's productive,
What renews and what will pass away, as seasons turn.
The rows and rows of cultivation measured and exact,
The panes of glass in wooden frames creating space enclosed
For growing things. The growing mind and thought of what can be
Sheltered in this building, this small building, relational
And made secure, a kind of generosity from owners.
A kind of dedication, of maintenance and sustenance, from occupants.

Autumn

And round it comes, no other way but this,
To mark the circle, but what disturbance
Threatening the cycle of renewal, now
Comes in to make the breakage
Permanent? Who would not mark
The seasons as they help?
Who would not oppose
The villainy of natural destruction?
The images and words attest
The music in the air across
A long time tells us, yes,
There is no other way but just to learn
How to attune not only mind but actions, to
The turning earth, the necessary rigours we are part of.

The Drains

Alex McCrindle, young honourable man,
              bringing his friends and fellows south, in 1961,
Comrades digging ditches there for drains,
                    to make the place more habitable, then
Training as an actor, grey-bearded after more than twenty years,
In Hollywood, surrounded by the *Star Wars* rebel forces in their earliest
Command,
      breathes out the phrase for that first time, in 1977:
'May the Force be with you!'
                  and he passes the energy on,
And disappears then, into the light.

Milne's Bar

The music from a city undersea,
The capital-in-waiting is itself a vast Cathedral,
The crown above St Giles, the castle on its dark volcanic plug,
Down the long slope of the mile, to the newest of designs, the parliament of Holyrood
And in one sweeping arc around,
Encompassing the new town of some centuries ago:
All of it a labyrinth, as any city must be,
And all of it beneath the deepest ocean: the air itself
Is Union. Inhabitants and denizens, citizens and subjects,
Who choose who they would wish to be, and swim within its atmosphere.
Its habitat assumes a British Empire. The Butcher's Apron flies upon its pole
Above it all, rising from the waters like a periscope,
Turning as the wind blows, here or there.

But deep within this undersea Cathedral,
There are some swimming people unpersuaded,
Who breathe by different means, whose gills are out of kilter with
Ascendancy of English, whose languages are different,
Gaelic, Scots, and flavoured with a music of a different kind and character.
Observe them swim through streets and wynds and alleyways,
Alone or in small shoals of three or five, chart them move as if upon a radar screen,
Or from the mappa mundi of the Outlook Tower:
Their currents turn and curve them, they come now towards a confluence,
A rendezvous approaches, somewhere in a dark and narrow street,
Run parallel to Princes Street, that broad, high-fronted, half-open shopping mall,
Commerce hard behind its walls and windows, outstretching to the gardens,
But with the Castle looming, and that serrated ridge of rooftops
Looking down from old town. Run parallel behind the brassy shopping,
There is a darker artery of blood: Rose Street: shadowy in summer, cool,
Both sinister and welcoming, dangerous and warm.

Milne's Bar. There at the corner, a short stone staircase takes you down
To further depths, beneath the city's sea. Go down these steps
And through this door and enter in
To this vast Cathedral's deepest vault.
The shadows thicken, multiply,
In depth and darkness.

Now the music that you heard so faintly from above it all begins to be
Articulate in voices, conversations, polyphonic, purposive, dynamics of
Communicative angles and directions of unknown approach.

And to the side, within the cavern now, another, smaller set of stairs
Leads further down, into the very crypt of this Cathedral. So let's go down.
And step by step,
                We do.
The sign is on the wall: this is the
'Little Kremlin'. The company we keep
Is here: the music of this whole encompassing
Cathedral undersea, has its source here.
We are in the thick of it, immersed in all its magic, now.
So listen, and, we'll hear what it says.
It flies to a different flag.
It touches the ear, enters through the cochlea,
Swims through the brain like a viral infection of health, an antidote to villainy.
Something is improving, getting better in the drift
Of swirling currents, vivid faces, gestures, love and carelessness
And sheer flamboyant fun,
As all the choral waters of the deep resistant world
Rise up through weights of water and oppression,
And filter out to atmospheres today, and politics yet, unwon.

DSCH

DSCH in Edinburgh, presiding at the moment,
Almost unrecorded:
Shostakovich, Stevenson and Grieve,
While radio and papers and the TV news
Had something else to say.
While held throughout the world in high esteem,
The Scottish press just treated him
Like some 'embarrassing joke'
And 'the English press ignored him' –
Thus said Alasdair Gray. 'Dunbar,
Burns, and MacDiarmid' was David Daiches's judgement:
'And of the three, MacDiarmid
Is the greatest miracle.'
What do we do these days with the miraculous?

Three men in suits, but, oh, what luminosity, colour, restraint,
Soothing and brightening, both.
In lock-down Soviet Russia,
In lock-down Scotland, 'coup of the mind',
In lock-down 2020,
Anyone might look out searchingly for colour.
Three men in suits:
RS, deliverer of gifts, a gift, a gift of honour given,
DSCH, acceptant, glowing, radiant in luminous red tie,
A saint of sorts, and CMG or HMacD, respectable and smart,
Demure, almost, placid as an undisturbed volcano,
Expressing neither confident assertion,
Nor the authority of pontification,
But there at the side,
Presiding as enabler, a man of strong
Encouragement, giving centre-stage to music, the passing
Of music from one beleaguered country to another.

A background blazing red is Leningrad in flames.
A yellow cyclorama of the unknown future sweeping round,
And the sense that even at the end,
What raises us all from despair
Will come through colour, texture,
Movement, such as this
Exemplifies:
This hard work of these three men in suits.

The unthinkable (Aberfan and Vietnam)

Nobody else would take the risk: the innocence of children,
All who care will know: that wee boy who drowned,
The children and their teachers buried
Under the sliding mountain of slag,
The piety of true remorse and anguish at our helplessness,
Our witnessing. And then he tells us, no,
We are not helpless. We tolerate. In fact,
We many of us still endorse, encourage, act
To make such horrors happen. Every TV news programme
You watch. Every paper you buy. In Vietnam the children die
So horribly, we cannot face comparison, and we deny
Complicity. We witness and we watch. It's spectacle,
And distanced. Compassion is the quickest thing,
And easily acknowledged, dealt with, moved on from.
The chilling hard ferocity, an analytic mind detached
From sentiment, refusing the manipulation
Of all the emotion directed, by media, which is to say,
By government, by law, by strict, enforced convention.
You go beyond the expectation. The shock is everlasting,
As it should be, faced with the catastrophe of fact:
This is what makes possible the murderous killing of infants.
A human response is more than feeling sad: it's seeing into causes,
Taking action to prevent them, doing what we can, still can,
And while we can. For each example shows, if the forces of control
Stay in control, our opposition cannot last forever.
Our manger faith is likely to be slaughtered,
As was theirs. We need this confrontation with the lie.

Y & MacD, GU, Bute Hall
from the places of abandonment

Monday, 10th November, 1975, the grand Bute Hall
In Glasgow University, packed with students, staff in some supply
But mainly students: Man of the moment, bathed
In adulation's spotlight: Yevtushenko on the stage,
Athletic, young, an advocate of seeing with fresh eyes,
Reading 'Babiy Yar' and speaking up for reading things again
Beyond the strictly guided points of view policed
By the elders. Nine years after Stalin. Beside him, Hugh MacDiarmid,
Scotland's Soviet Commissar, kilted, grey, his hair at full attention and salute,
Figure of disdain and popular derision, old codger to a generation
Tuning in intensely to whatever was Top of the Pops.
But that's not what I saw. What I saw was this apparatchik,
Playing to the gallery, and standing there beside him,
This veteran of two world wars, who'd seen what death and devastation mean
And knew what cold and poverty and isolation, desolation, felt like,
Speaking from a depth of sheer conviction
And a strength born out of all of life most vulnerable,
Doing his job, then folding the papers away.

Brownsbank domesticity

Two rooms: it was a partnership,
>   sustained by separation
>>   and each the other's company.

His, the wall above around the fireplace, portraits:
'A growing shrine to my vanity,' he said – but truly?
Did he ever look at them? Loveday, Coia, Kitaj?
The photographs? Or somewhere unacknowledged
Was a gratitude for confirmation needed?
That writers need the readers they respect and write for,
Not a sea of critics they despise, nor a mob of ignorance
Made volatile and goaded into practice of reflexive denigration,
By those prevailing attitudes, which cannot comprehend
Whatever they arise from, or that which they seek to convey:
Fashion, commercialism, bestsellers and books of the week.
>   'The poet a Tarzan among apes, all
>   Suddenly, murderously, inimical.'

Time slows. Patience is more than required. Wait. And then see.
>   Pipes on the mantelpiece. A clock. A radio tuned to the news.
>>   His papers, pens, his shelved collection of paperback crim

The glass-fronted doors of the cabinet, with his own books, safely stored,
A whisky bottle on its top, and, beside his chair,
The stockpiled copies of the *Morning Star*.
>>   Hers, Cornwall:

D.H. Lawrence, A.L. Rowse, fishing floats and packets,
Jars, of henna, Nescafé,

                The TV in the corner by the windowsill
And telephone, brass decorative horse rings, hanging by the wall.
(He would not have any if the image of Churchill was on them.)
It's like this now. It was like this then, when I was there.

An old man doing such domestic jobs
                as washing dishes after every meal,
with firm attention, CMG, his knuckles,
                    fingers, gently, firmly bent around
the cutlery and crockery in soapy water,
              then the drying, putting away,
for use next time,
                  the conservation of the effort needed.
His face intent, gaze down, giving it attention.
           'Not the job accepted by most men
in that day's patriarchal ethos.'
              His shuffling walk, from sitting room
to kitchen and then back, to sit and
      then to carefully,
           resume the conversation,
                  whoever the company was.

Valda's poem

If he had not been helpless and so ready
To light her cigarette just as he did,
Had been as certain as he was in fact,
And acted like a man in charge, instead
Of all that made her charmed and charming,
That changed her independence to protectiveness,
It would not have gone the way it did, it could not
Have sparked and kindled, love, to love, not as it were
To be 'in love' (that drunk romantic thing, excess
Of feeling) but love, which is to care and care for,
Open-eyed and sometimes recognising failing,
Failures, misdirected lines, misapplications
Of our energies, those old desires we think we have
And know so little of until we try them once again, and then,
Return to this: a fact of this commitment, now,
Sustained through years and decades of a hardship still
To many simply unimagined, a nexus of connection,
Most look on and might feel quite nothing of. But in that home,
Protection was the rule. To judge with care and hard
Discrimination, who to allow to enter through that door,
To whom that postcard should be returned, unstamped,
The hypocrites surrounding them, rejected, and the friends,
Welcomed, family, the Irish wheaten terriers, the dogs,
The close friends going with her on the holidays
On package tours to Spain, or back to Cornwall.
The garden to be tended in due season.

Tait's MacDiarmid

Piano notes, forthright, and chords, both bold and curious,

then song, a voice, a Scots voice, opening the air.

And in the air, there, also, there is The Voice of the BBC

on radio waves, the information, properly, official and approved –

(beside the books of poems, information, unofficial, edged, the wedge) –

a radio, newspapers, poems and songs:
                                      What might you do, unorthodox,

against time and within it, measured and spontaneous, delicate and strong?

The vision moves
                     along the clocks where they sit on the mantlepiece,

as their long and short hands move, around, then the vision moves

back along the other way,

       and it slows you down to see that:

time moving, the fire in the hearth, burning, the grate,

and there, in the light on the shelves by the window,

the pot plants growing in their earth containments.

A man on the edge of a pavement,

on the rim of the squared slabs, balancing between

the raised stone platform by the road and

all its passing traffic, then stepping up and

walking on a wall, or down a set of stone steps,

stepping, down, leaning, swaying, then weighing back,

going down to the edge of the sea, by the rippling waves,

the dark encroaching waters of the sea, the man

throwing stones into the sea –

A glimmer of laughter, a ripple of his shoulders,
neck down, head dipped, a dodge, a piece of cheek
or mischief, disguising an accomplishment unspoken.

The door to the house opens.
He goes in. The door closes.

The thick carved wooden knocker is there
on the outside of the closed door.

The light goes on through the window,
the curtains are open – there is the unseen,
there is the invitation of the visible –
The multitude of books, inside!
The film by which we see them.

Afterwords

Coda

The lunatic, the lover and the poet –
What madness reigns and what fanatic zeal
Or uttermost despondency, what icy depths, what cold
Of unremitting distance and command? What care,
Attention, intuitive knowledge, sympathetic grasp,
Imagination's ecstasy, material touch and taste,
The physic of that physicality, what bodies are and what
This body is. The work of the accord that writing brings
When source and delivery, sustenance and strength
Are kept in balance here, this godly and ungodly world,
These three in one, these multitudes of meanings:
Are of imagination all compact –

Elegy

We travelled very quickly and suddenly stopped
In a world far different from that we had left –

In forest glade, in the cemetery, gently,
Trees breathe and brush, leaves and branches wave –

In the grass, an indented rectangle
Extends from your headstone, over your grave –

Earth is residual, for better or worse,
There's darkness in the soil and patience in the well –

Rivers sound their secrets all around us
And above in the night air, meteors fly –

MacDiarmid's Language
(after Charles Olson)

You can see
MacDiarmid's language
advancing
In directions of production
which were probably never guessed
at; and which symbols and allegories
are evidences of, no more unusual
than the substance
needed for them to work.

     Aid and abetment
to help recognition of forms
     'weak' in proportion
to the size of the substance.

(That is, for a rose to fall
for the trees
to blaze in Autumn for the
missing, for the rivers to unsound
their secrets and come down, it takes
the earth, even in this
sophisticated society.

Notes

Dedication

The quotation after the dedication comes from a BBC radio programme, 'A Tribute in Memory of Hugh MacDiarmid', which I listened to and recorded when it was broadcast, on the day of his death, 9 September 1978.

Discretions

The sources for these epigraphs are: Hugh MacDiarmid, *Lucky Poet: A Self-Study in Literature and Political Ideas* (London: Jonathan Cape, 1943; reprinted Carcanet, 1994); Hugh MacDiarmid 'Scotland: Full Circle', in Duncan Glen, ed., *Whither Scotland? A prejudiced look at the future of a nation* (London: Victor Gollancz, 1971); Salman Rushdie, *The Satanic Verses* (London: Viking, 1988); Wole Soyinka, 'New Frontiers for Old' (1990), in *Art, Dialogue and Outrage: Essays on Literature and Culture* (London: Methuen, 1993); Adrienne Rich, *Poetry and Commitment: An Essay* (New York: W.W. Norton, 2007), first presented as the plenary lecture at the 2006 Conference on Poetry and Politics, Stirling University, Scotland; Elizabeth Melville, Lady Culross, *Poems: Unpublished work from manuscript with 'Ane Godlie Dreme'*, edited by Jamie Reid Baxter (Edinburgh: Solsequium, 2010); William Blake, *The Marriage of Heaven and Hell*, edited by Michael Phillips (Oxford: The Bodleian Library, 2011).

Three Rivers

Bill Vevers, editor, *Hugh MacDiarmid: The Langholm and Eskdale Connection* (Langholm: Littles, 1985); Alex Carruthers, *Walking with Wanderer: Exploring the Hills around Langholm* (Langholm: The Langholm Initiative, 2000); John Hyslop, and his son Robert Hyslop, revised by Robert Hyslop's granddaughter Dorothy Hyslop Booth and great-grandson Ewan D. Booth, *Langholm As It Was: A History of Langholm and Eskdale from the Earliest Times* (Inverness: D.H. Booth & E.D. Booth, 2002); John H. Gair, *Langholm and the Surrounding Area Through the Ages* (Langholm: Langholm Archive Group, c.2007).

The learning

The words of the Anglican hymn 'All Things Bright and Beautiful' are by the Anglo-Irish Cecil Frances Alexander, first published in her *Hymns for Little Children* (1848), usually sung to the tune composed by William Henry Monck in 1887. The sense that God made heaven and earth and the natural world in its entirety may have been suggested by Psalm 104, verses 24 and 25: 'Oh Lord, how manifold are thy works! in wisdom hast thou made them all: the earth is full of thy riches. So is this great and wide sea, wherein are things creeping innumerable, both small and great beasts.' And also, perhaps, by Coleridge's 'The Rime of the Ancient Mariner': 'He prayeth best, who loveth best; / All things great and small; / For the dear God who loveth us; / He made and loveth all.' Or perhaps from William Paley's *Natural Theology* (1802), where God is the designer of the natural world, the Divine Watchmaker. Alexander may also have had particular locations in mind, in Wales, Ireland and England, but probably not in Scotland. The third verse refers to 'The rich man in his castle, / The poor man at his gate' implying that social hierarchy is also God-ordained, a hard thought at the time of the Irish and Scottish Famines of the 1840s. Alexander had been brought up in the world of a land-agent on an Irish estate. The ironies are all there but the wonder of creation, the manger-faith in life, is as profound as it is childish, and MacDiarmid has it too. He begins one of the poems entitled 'Scotland' with the lines: 'It requires great love of it, deeply to read / The configuration of a land…' But with him, there's no concealment of hypocrisies: exposure is unending, for creation is never fulfilled. And in childhood, it's only beginning.

The Purchase of Tarras Moor

See: https://www.langholminitiative.org.uk/

The Library

Hugh MacDiarmid, *Lucky Poet: A Self-Study in Literature and Political Ideas* (London: Jonathan Cape, 1943), p.8: 'It was that library, however, that was the great determining factor...I had constant access to it, and used to fill a big washing-basket with books and bring it downstairs as often as I wanted to. My parents never interfered with or supervised my reading in any way, nor were they ever in the least inclined to deprecate my "wasting all my time reading". There were upwards of twelve thousand books in the library (though it was strangely deficient in Scottish books), and a fair number of new books, chiefly novels, was constantly bought. Before I left home (when I was fourteen) I could go up into that library in the dark and find any book I wanted. I could do so still if the arrangement of the shelves has not been altered, although I have not been in it for thirty years now; and I can still remember not only where about on the shelves all sorts of books were, but whereabouts in the books themselves were favourite passages or portions that interested me specially for one reason or another, so that I could go straight to them and open them – hundreds of them – at or about the very place in question.' MacDiarmid says he left home at age fourteen but both biographies by Gordon Wright and Alan Bold have him departing for Broughton in 1908, when he would have been sixteen. See also Ruth McQuillan, 'Langholm Library', *Akros* (vol.9, no.25, August 1974).

The Ministry of Water

Nancy K. Gish, *Hugh MacDiarmid: The Man and His Work* (London: Macmillan, 1984), especially Chapter 1: Borderer and Exile, p.14.

The Border Guards

'Nervous, highly strung, tautly sensitive with quick reactions, [Francis George Scott] had a powerful brain and was fortunate in that he needed little sleep so that he could work a twenty-four-hour-day, showing not the slightest sign of fatigue. Francis taught me with enthusiasm. He became greatly excited by what he saw as the possibility of a splendid revival, a Scottish Renaissance of the arts. We three were to be the core of this Renaissance. He felt that if we all pulled our weight together and tried, Christopher with his poetry, I with my painting and Francis with his music, all having a revolutionary point of view, we could raise the standard of the arts right from the gutter into something that would be really important. He thought that it was a great coincidence that there were three of us, all from the Borders, interested in a great resurgence of art in Scotland'. – William Johnstone, *Points in Time: An Autobiography* (London: Barrie and Jenkins, 1980), p.72. F.G. Scott, *Moonstruck: Songs of F.G. Scott*, Lisa Milne, soprano; Roderick Williams, baritone; Iain Burnside, piano (Signum Classics, SIGCD096, 2007); F.G. Scott, *Complete Music for Solo Piano*, Christopher Guild, piano (Toccata Classics: TOCC 0547, 2021).

The Scottish Soul

Nancy K. Gish, Hugh MacDiarmid: The Man and His Work (London: Macmillan, 1984), especially Chapter 1: Borderer and Exile, pp.7-8.

Cultural Appropriation

'There are certain voyage stops – like the bookmark – inscribed into any attempt to review the world's accounting of a receding millennium, stops that are likely to remain pertinent to succeeding generations, and for centuries. Most individuals have their sobering lists, a mere recollection of which checks them in stride even in the midst of marveling or celebrating the undeniable, often unthinkable leaps in human achievements. It would be astonishing if the average list does not contain one or both of the following: the Holocaust and Hiroshima. For most Africans at home or dispersed, however, there is a third. […] The third [is] a far more elusive, insidious, and seemingly eternal condition. It is also, paradoxically, a self-attenuating metaphor, which perhaps accounts for its tenacity, since it encourages a tendency toward toleration. […] The third offers evidence not even of the short memory of the world but of the regard with which the African continent is held, since it is one that would leap instantly to the head of a list for the average African. By contrast, it would have to be near forcefully impressed on others as a candidate for such a list. I have encountered this cast of mind – that is, requiring re-education, at several gatherings devoted to Memory, Race Relations, Human Rights, Conflict Resolution, Reconciliation Strategies – and allied themes. It is indeed revealing of much else, since this third bookmark happens to lack the consolation of being in a terminal past – unlike the Holocaust or Hiroshima, it lacks an identifiably limited duration. […] Yes, indeed, we have in mind the African slave trade.' – Wole Soyinka, *Of Africa* (New Haven and London: Yale University Press, 2012), pp.54-56. There is slavery of the body. There is slavery of the mind.

Europe's far enough for me

Alexander Linklater suggested to me that MacDiarmid's writings about the First World War had relatively little directly to do with his own personal experiences. Which really changes nothing. Was it what he did, or just what he imagined? Linklater specifies that the sketch entitled 'Casualties', published as part of C.M. Grieve's first book, *Annals of the Five Senses* (1923), 'superficially appears to draw on his experiences in the Royal Army Medical Corps. However, the scene he describes takes place in the muddy trenches of the Somme, where CMG has never been, rather than the malarial heat of Salonika, in which, at that moment, he is languishing.' When he sent the sketch to his erstwhile schoolteacher, George Ogilvie, Grieve made no remark on what Linklater calls this 'bizarre incongruity'. But sometimes imagination is worse than real experience. Experience comes to an end. The endlessness of what a mind can think of is sometimes more frightening. So we might imagine him, imagining this. And if the idea of the 'small nation' only meant that any small nation is at the mercy of a larger empire, then yes, such a nation would be far too small indeed, and overrun too easily and quickly by hostile ideologies. But diversity is the other side of dividedness, so there is then another kind of opposition: warfare declared between the force of empires of the mind in conflict: on one side, endlessness, enquiry, richness of identities, of languages, terrains and peoples, a principle of exploration, sensitisation. And on the other side: uniformity, the authority of rule and strict suppression. Numbness. The desensitised self. How are we to oppose this battleground of Europe? And how can Scotland be imagined in it?

Renaissance

Duncan Glen, *Hugh MacDiarmid and the Scottish Renaissance* (Edinburgh: Chambers, 1964). One of the earliest and best pioneering expeditions into the field and opening the sheer extent of it.

Vortex

The 'night of the assembly' refers to the construction of *A Drunk Man Looks at the Thistle*, which seems to have taken place in a holiday bungalow named 'Avondale' in St Cyrus, near Montrose, where F.G. Scott visited C.M. Grieve while his wife Peggy and their children were away, in the summer of 1926. My thanks to Andy Shanks, formerly Head Teacher at Montrose Academy, for suggesting this to me. See also Kathleen Jamie, 'The Way We Live', in *Mr and Mrs Scotland Are Dead: Poems 1980-1994* (Tarset, Northumberland: Bloodaxe Books, 2002), p.76.

Company / Home / Love & loss

Alan Bold, MacDiarmid: *Christopher Murray Grieve, A Critical Biography* (London: John Murray, 1988; Paladin Books, 1990). For 'Company' see also Robert Creeley, 'I Know a Man', in *Poems 1950-1965* (London: Calder and Boyars 1966), p.38.

Prelude to Shetland

Helen Burness Cruickshank, 'Mainly Domestic: Being some Personal Reminiscences', in *MacDiarmid: A Festschrift*, edited by K.D. Duval and Sydney Goodsir Smith (Edinburgh: K.D. Duval, 1962); Helen B. Cruickshank, *Octobiography* (Montrose: The Standard Press, 1976).

MacDiarmid on Whalsay: A Glass of Cold Water, Mid-Afternoon, Air Salt Stone, Valda and Michael

Laurence Graham and Brian Smith, editors, *MacDiarmid in Shetland* (Lerwick: Shetland Library, 1992), especially Michael Grieve,

'Foreword' and Brian Smith, 'Stony Limits: the Grieves in Whalsay, 1933-1942'; Gordon Wright, *MacDiarmid: An Illustrated Biography* (Edinburgh: Gordon Wright, 1977).

MI5

Andrew McNeillie, 'Spying on MacDiarmid', *The Times Literary Supplement*, 13 September 2013, pp.14-15; Scott Lyall, 'Hugh MacDiarmid and the British State', *The Bottle Imp*, Issue 18 (Glasgow: ASLS, June 2015).

With the fishermen

Ruth McQuillan, *In line with the Ramna Stacks: A study of the fishing poems of Hugh MacDiarmid* (Edinburgh: Challister Press, 1981); Ruth McQuillan, 'MacDiarmid's Shetland Poetry', in Laurence Graham and Brian Smith, editors, *MacDiarmid in Shetland* (Lerwick: Shetland Library, 1992).

Technique & Ideation

The phrase 'technique and ideation' appears in 'The Chapbook Programme', in *The Scottish Chapbook* (vol.1, no.1, August 1922), which is republished as 'A New Movement in Scottish Literature', in MacDiarmid's *Selected Prose*, ed. Alan Riach (Manchester: Carcanet, 1992), pp.3-8 (p.5) and cited in Margery Palmer McCulloch (ed.), *Modernism and Nationalism: Literature and Society in Scotland 1918-1939, Source Documents for the Scottish Renaissance* (Glasgow: ASLS, 2004), p.xii.

Onwards

The imagery of molten metal reforming itself is from James Cameron's film *Terminator 2: Judgement Day* (1991).

The lines of men

'Beckett's line' is that the survivor has one further suffering to go through beyond the one who suffers and dies: that is the suffering of the witness. It comes from his early essay on Proust: 'pity for what has been suffered is a more cruel and precise expression for that suffering than the conscious estimate of the sufferer, who is spared at least one despair – the despair of the spectator.' It's quoted in Adrian Poole's *Tragedy: Shakespeare and the Greek Example* (Oxford: Basil Blackwell, 1987), where Poole comments: 'Tragedy is founded on the relationship between sufferer and spectator, on what passes between them – between "us" who are going to be left behind in this harsh world to draw our breath in pain, as Horatio is at the end of *Hamlet*, and "him" or "her" or "them" who is or are leaving it.'

There's some truth in that, and Poole is right to emphasise Beckett's perception: 'There is a chill in that shudder from "spare" to "despair": the sufferer is "spared" the "despair" of the spectator, as if "to spare" and "to despair" were cognate. There is a cruelty in the anger and pity which tragedy arouses in the spectator, as St Augustine recognised, a cruelty in the feelings aroused by the representation of sufferings that you cannot do anything about. As readers or audience we attend diversely to the beings on stage who suffer and pity and rage. And through the forms which these beings take and make, we recognise both individually and collectively the diversities in ourselves, in the communities to which we belong, and in our world. In this we are at one.'

And yet, the despair of the witness, looking on at the spectacle of the 'lines of men' going into a second world war, is held in balance against the knowledge that many, perhaps most, of those men will not be spared. It's painful knowledge, but yet a value, remaining, when the loss is irrevocable. And that loss may be more than men: it may be a language, a species, cultural identity in complexities, all forms of expression possible to all of us aware of what Poole calls 'the diversities in ourselves'. St Augustine was wrong: cruelty may not be present in the feelings of the helpless witness, and if it is, there are other feelings too, like disgust, contempt, and anger, not for the sufferers but for who and what have brought them to this.

The World Language

In his essay, 'What I Believe', in *The Writer at Work: Essays* (Dunedin: University of Otago Press, 2000), pp.200-206, C.K. Stead says this: 'A discussion of what one believes usually begins or leads to the question of "God". "Do you believe in God?" Through many European centuries it has been at least socially unacceptable, often dangerous, and sometimes suicidal, to answer in the negative. The freedom to answer is therefore something to be affirmed and protected: and if I am to give a short answer, that is what mine must be.' Which is fair enough, but not quite enough. Stead goes on: 'My dislike of the short rough answer springs, not from uncertainty, but from a disinclination to give the question the status, which such an answer confers, of something entirely meaningful. What am I saying I don't believe in if my answer is no? To concede that one understands this is to turn the negative into a form of denial: "God may exist but I refuse to believe it." I prefer to see "God" as a word to which there is nothing objective corresponding – a word which usage over time slowly defined, and then knowledge over time rendered a nonsense.'

That seems to me an important distinction. How much of what most people accept is simply repeated fiction? Of all poets, MacDiarmid was most keenly aware of the political significance of this. But fictions can yield truths: the music of Bach, the cathedrals of Chartres and Amiens, the poetry of Hopkins and Donne. Stead's conclusion seems pertinent too: 'I know, and accord qualified respect to, the traditions which pertain to the word. I see no reason to question the authenticity of subjective experiences which many distinguished, and many more undistinguished, persons have reported, and which give the word force and significance in their lives. That tells me something about the human psyche and about how language works; it tells me nothing at all about the larger facts of the universe we occupy. If every person in the world believed the moon was made of green cheese that would not make it so. So my intellectual position is subtly, but I think significantly, different from both atheism and agnosticism. The atheist denies God exists; the agnostic doesn't know. For me the word "God" lacks a referent; lacks objective meaning; and consequently uncertainty about, or denial of, God's "existence" are equally without meaning.'

I'd agree with that but it isn't quite how MacDiarmid uses the word, either in his poems or in the essay from which the epigraph to the poem 'The World Language' in this book is taken. Rather, MacDiarmid uses the word as a metaphor for the most extended and encompassing consciousness human beings might imagine. It is clearly not a human consciousness for MacDiarmid's proposition is of immortality. So both 'God' and 'immortality' in his imagining are metaphoric words giving human beings means of measuring value in a changing world. Stead's observations on the word 'God' are especially useful if we want to historicise and analyse MacDiarmid's work and his use of the word, whatever we may think ourselves. They might also help clarify our own thinking about the word. And this challenge to our own habits, forms and assumptions of thought is what we have to deal with when we read MacDiarmid.

Cottage

Scarcely Ever Out of My Thoughts: The Letters of Valda Trevlyn Grieve to Christopher Murray Grieve (Hugh MacDiarmid), edited by Beth Junor, with a Foreword by Deirdre Grieve (Edinburgh: Word Power Books, 2007).

The Seasons: Winter, Spring and Summer, Autumn

These poems were written directly in response to Ruth Nicol's paintings.

The Drains

There's one further affectionate connection I have with Alex McCrindle. It was the very first ever professional theatrical play I ever saw, was taken to by my father, in March 1974, at the Old Vic in London, the National Theatre production of Shakespeare's *The Tempest,* with John Gielgud as Prospero and Jenny Agutter as Miranda and a cast that included Cyril Cusack, Arthur Lowe, Julian Orchard, in a show that was pure magic, all through, from the shapes and voices so vivid in the conjuring that I could never work out how they appeared as they did, to Ariel, zipping around the space above the stage with no sign of anything except him flying, and Gielgud and Agutter doing everything only they could have done, there and then, and the first scene is a storm at sea, and it was wild, lightning, rain, howling, thunder, the ship's deck, masts, sails, ocean rising, crashing, all of it – and Alex McCrindle was playing the ship's captain, 'The Master of a ship' and in all that whirlwind action I still remember him, his movements, voice and command. It's strange to think how that memory has stayed with me – nearly half a century, from then till the writing of this!

Milne's Bar

MacDiarmid's poem 'Homage to Dunbar' talks of the sounds of the bells of Ys, as if from a cathedral undersea, reaching at times to a strange and distant ear, that can hear, far off, the music of a sunken place, that still wins through, despite all else, or may, just, be able to, even yet. The poem was written directly in response to Sandy Moffat's painting.

DSCH

Ronald Stevenson, *Passacaglia on DSCH, Recitative and Air for Dmitri Shostakovich, Prelude, Fugue and Fantasy on themes from Busoni's Doctor Faust,* Ronald Stevenson, piano (Altarus, AIR-CD-9091, 1989); Ronald Stevenson, *Passacaglia and Dmitri Shostakovich, Preludes and Fugues, On DSCH*, Igor Levit, piano (Sony Classical, 2021). See also Tom Buchan, 'Scotland the wee', in *Dolphins at Cochin* (London: Barrie & Rockliff / The Cresset Press, 1969). This poem was written in response to Sandy's painting but with Ronald's music very much in my mind.

The unthinkable (Aberfan and Vietnam)

The disaster at Aberfan, four miles south of Merthyr Tydfil, in Wales, occurred on 21 October 1966, when a colliery spoil tip collapsed and slipped downhill onto homes and a school, killing 116 children and 28 adults. The number of deaths of children caused by military intervention in Vietnam is not securely calculable.

YY & MacD, GU, Bute Hall

This is Marshall Walker's recollection, as he told me what he saw at the event, a witness. He was in the English Department at Glasgow University when the reading took place. And he was my friend and colleague and comrade at the University of Waikato, New Zealand, from 1986 to 2000, and the author of *Scottish Literature since 1707* (Harlow: Longman, 1996) and *Dear Sibelius: Letter from a Junky* (Glasgow: Kennedy & Boyd, 2008).

Brownsbank domesticity

I'm indebted to Jackie Kay for pointing out to me that C.M. Grieve's willing undertaking of domestic responsibilities like the washing-up was fairly unusual in that patriarchal era. There are various aspects of the lives of Valda and Chris I can illustrate here. On one occasion when I arrived to visit, having taken my time driving over the border hills enjoying the landscape in the sunny afternoon, Valda met me at the door: 'You're late!' she pronounced, and proceeded to bundle me back into the car, to drive her into Biggar to the bank before it closed, to pick up her travellers' cheques before she left on a package tour to Spain the following morning. The bank was shut. There was no hesitation. Straight from the car, up the path, to hammer on the big wooden door till it opened and she was admitted, her cheques handed over to her, and then back to Brownsbank for my appointed conversation with Christopher.

William Grant and Sons Ltd., the Scotch whisky distillers, created the honorary position of 'Governor of the Academy of Pure Malt Scotch Whisky to create knowledge and understanding of pure malt Scotch whisky' and Christopher was one of seven distinguished men invited to occupy this role. When I visited, an ample supply of Glenfiddich helped fuel our conversation and I remember that at one point the discussion trifurcated in the pursuit of three subjects: the quality of Turkish tobacco, the original breeding of poodles as hunting dogs and the poetry of the great Victorian Charles M. Doughty, author of

The Dawn in Britain, Adam Cast Forth and *Travels in Arabia Deserta.* Christopher told me of a visit he had made to Cambridge, to Downing College, whose Charles Doughty Society had invited him knowing that he had written an essay and a magnificent elegy for Doughty. 'Strangely enough,' he told me, 'at Downing College, there was a rule that no alcohol should be consumed on the premises other than sherry. I don't know if you're aware of this, Alan, but sherry is…' his brow beetled a bit and he scowled a little, 'a kind of *wine*.' I said yes, I was aware of that. 'Well,' he puffed his pipe. 'There were three hundred bottles of sherry consumed that evening after my talk, and I was feeling a little queasy.' I agreed that I could imagine how that might be so. 'Then I remembered – my old friend David Daiches was in the college across the road, so I went over and knocked on his door, and he opened it, and I asked if he had any malt whisky. He did, and we drank it. That settled my stomach, and I was fine after that.'

Many years later, I told this story to David Daiches. He smiled fondly. 'It's true,' he said. 'I remember it vividly. It was Glenmorangie. I've never seen a man so glad to see a bottle of whisky.'

In Brownsbank that time, after a couple of hours, the conversation had returned to Doughty when Valda joined us, coming through from her room, going into the kitchen having seen us in full engagement, then returning to stand in the doorway, to interrupt the flow of words and Glenfiddich with, 'Well, I can't talk to you about Victorian epic poetry, but would you like a fried egg roll or a bacon roll?' Before she could finish the sentence, Chris had interrupted her: 'You have nothing but laziness and ignorance to conquer!'

Affection was there all right, but stronger was the sense that practice keeps the edges sharp. She sighed, we agreed about food, tea to wash it down with, and went on.

When one of their dogs, Clootie, an Irish Wheaten Terrier, approached my right ankle with a cheeky yelp, I reached down tentatively to pat it on the head. 'I wouldn't do that, if I were you!' Valda called from the doorway. 'That one kills sheep!' It turned to Chris, sharp teeth and expectancy. His expression was severe as stone. He took a copy of the *Morning Star* from the top of the high pile between his chair and the fireplace, rolled it up into a stiff bludgeon and held it poised above the little dog. It skulked off.

I was told the following anecdote by Norman MacCaig and have no reason to doubt it: one evening, Chris working, writing deep in concentration, Valda decided to go to bed and tells him to remember to put out the empty milk bottles. Job completed, Chris can't remember what she's told him, but remembers something. Next morning,the milkman finds on the doorstep a glass of water with Chris's false teeth in it.

Tait's MacDiarmid

Margaret Tait, *Hugh MacDiarmid: A Portrait* (Ancona Films, 1964).

Valda's poem

Returning an unstamped postcard or even a Christmas card to the sender who had offended her was the mildest of Valda's rebukes. She told me once that when she was a wee girl, she'd been instructed not to visit the old woman who lived at the end of the road because she was a witch. Of course, she went and visited as soon as she could smuggle herself out of the house when no-one was looking, and the old lady taught her a Cornish curse and made her swear to never repeat it. Valda told me she'd used it twice. The first time, she said, she cursed the artist R.H. Westwater, whose portrait of MacDiarmid is on the cover of the first Penguin edition of the *Selected Poems* and is held by the National Portrait Gallery in Edinburgh. She told me that when Chris had visited to sit for the portrait, Westwater had encouraged him to drink and had been talking of suicide, and when Chris returned home, he was quite drunk and was talking of suicide. Valda was enraged and cursed the artist. 'What happened?' I asked. She replied, 'Very soon afterwards, he died.' I paused and drew breath and asked then, 'And the second time?' She smiled and said, 'Maurice Lindsay.' This was probably in the mid-1980s. 'But Valda,' I said, 'Maurice is still with us.' She smiled more broadly and said, 'Yes, but the week after I cursed him, the roof of his house blew off.' She was a serious character.

Coda

The first and last lines are from *A Midsummer Night's Dream,* of course.

Elegy

Some of these poems are works of the imagination. This is not.

MacDiarmid's Language

This is based on Charles Olson's poem '"Ed Sanders' Language"' which I read in *Additional Prose: A Bibliography on America, Proprioception & Other Notes & Essays* (Bolinas: Four Seasons Foundation, 1974). It is reprinted in *Collected Prose by Charles Olson* (Berkeley: University of California Press, 1997). My poem uses certain of Olson's lines and phrases, and it suggests an affinity between the poetic indications of the future purpose of language coming from all three poets' understanding of the past. Hopefully, it connects Olson and MacDiarmid in the dimension of imagination which had already been suggested by Olson himself, in his notes dated June 22, 1955, for a tutorial on the Greeks he gave at Black Mountain College, North Carolina, collected in *Olson: The Journal of the Charles Olson Archives* (no.2, Fall 1974, p.44): 'The 3rd cent. BC is also a gallery. For example, there is a lovely homosexual poet (an Alexandrian!) who must date from this century who did a damned fresh poem on Orpheus' death (such Alexandrians have approximately the relation to great Greeks as the Scots do to the English, like that Scot now, and Dunbar etc. after Chaucer). – I am not sure, however, if the 3rd Cent. BC is as relevant overall as the 2nd AD. But T heocritus is enuf to suggest more. Poke around in it.' Copies among the papers of Edward Dorn and Michael Rumaker suggest they had been made available to Black Mountain students. Olson's painstaking editor, George F. Butterick, noted that the Alexandrian poet was probably Phanocles and explains the reference to 'that Scot now' as 'The poet Hugh MacDiarmid'. In a personal letter dated 3 April 1985, George Butterick informed me that the only book by MacDiarmid in Olson's library was *In Memoriam James Joyce*, the second impression from 1956, and commented that although there was no further evidence that Olson had read MacDiarmid, 'one knows strongly, intuitively he must have approved of him utterly. Their sense of the "local" in language, for one thing.' It's a good thought, to confirm even a speculative recognition of such an intrinsic affinity. I hope my poem endorses it. It is published with the kind approval of the University of Connecticut and the Estate of Charles Olson.

The MacDiarmid Memorandum: Biographies

HUGH MACDIARMID (Christopher Murray Grieve, 1892-1978) was a major poet and cultural revolutionary, the inspirational leader at the head of the Scottish Renaissance of the 1920s, a rejuvenation of culture, politics and national potential. From helping found the National Party of Scotland and writing a lifetime of work including *A Drunk Man Looks at the Thistle* (1926), *Stony Limits* (1935) and *In Memoriam James Joyce* (1955), his impact was and is charged with a dynamic power that rebukes authority and yet commands it.

ALAN RIACH is Professor of Scottish Literature at the University of Glasgow, the author of eight poetry collections, including *Homecoming* and *The Winter Book*, six books of literary and cultural criticism, the General Editor of the Carcanet edition of the *Collected Works of Hugh MacDiarmid* and author of *Hugh MacDiarmid's Epic Poetry*, *Scottish Literature: An Introduction*, and co-author with Alexander Moffat of *Arts of Resistance: Poets, Portraits and Landscapes of Modern Scotland*.

ALEXANDER MOFFAT is a painter, teacher and advocate of the arts, formerly head of Painting at Glasgow School of Art, whose works are held at the National Galleries of Scotland, the University of Edinburgh, the University of Glasgow and the Royal Scottish Academy. His iconic group-portrait *Poets' Pub* (1982) is held in the National Portrait Gallery, Edinburgh. Its complementary epic group portrait *Scotland's Voices* (2017) depicts the singers and musicians of the oral tradition.

RUTH NICOL is an artist whose work has been exhibited throughout Scotland and is represented by the Open Eye Gallery, Edinburgh, the Line Gallery, Linlithgow and the Junor Gallery, St Andrews, and is regularly shown at the Royal Scottish Academy, the Royal Glasgow Institute and Paisley Art Institute. Her major Edinburgh panorama landscape *Holyrood, 2014* is held in the Scottish Parliament.

WILLIAM JOHNSTONE (1897-1981) was a major artist, teacher and farmer. His early Borders landscapes and portraits evolved after periods in Colorado and Arizona studying native American art and he became a pioneer of Scottish abstract art. The National Galleries of Scotland hold *A Point in Time* (1929-37). Some of his later pen-and-wash drawings were published to accompany poems by his friend Hugh MacDiarmid. He was the cousin of the composer Francis George Scott.

DEIRDRE GRIEVE (Deirdre Chapman) is a writer, former journalist and newspaper columnist, and was the daughter-in-law of Hugh MacDiarmid and Valda Trevlyn, married to Michael Grieve (1932-95), with whom she had three sons, Christopher (b.1960), Lucien (b.1964) and Dorian (b.1973).

RONALD STEVENSON (1928-2015) was a major composer, virtuoso pianist, teacher, close friend of MacDiarmid, advocate of the arts and encourager of artists, whose epic piano composition *Passacaglia on DSCH* (1962) has been recorded to high critical acclaim by Igor Levit and whose song-settings of MacDiarmid and many others, along with other full-scale and miniature musical compositions, are available on numerous CDs, including the incomparable 'Ae Gowden Lyric'.